WENDY DALRYMPLE

Parasocial

Copyright © 2023 by Wendy Dalrymple

All rights reserved. No part of this publication may be reproduced, stored or transmitted in any form or by any means, electronic, mechanical, photocopying, recording, scanning, or otherwise without written permission from the publisher. It is illegal to copy this book, post it to a website, or distribute it by any other means without permission.

First edition

*This book was professionally typeset on Reedsy.
Find out more at reedsy.com*

Contents

Foreword	iv
Chapter One	1
Chapter Two	9
Chapter Three	18
Chapter Four	25
Chapter Five	32
Chapter Six	38
Chapter Seven	46
Chapter Eight	53
Chapter Nine	61
Chapter Ten	67
Chapter Eleven	75
Chapter Twelve	82
Chapter Thirteen	89
Chapter Fourteen	94
Chapter Fifteen	98
About the Author	105
Also by Wendy Dalrymple	106

Foreword

Parasocial [par-uh-soh-shuhl] relationship: The connection, or imagined connection, between a regular person and a fictional character, celebrity, or other person.

Chapter One

What makes the basis of a friendship anyway? Is a relationship between two people only considered a true friendship when a declaration is made? Does a person have to actually meet someone face-to-face to be considered a true friend? Do you have to share the same air, walk the same path, engage in direct eye contact? Or, when it comes to friends, is there something more?

I believed there was. There was something intangible that couldn't quite be named between two people who loved each other platonically, an invisible thread that connected one to another through space and time. This was how I felt about Della, and I was certain that was how she felt about me.

Della had over 624K followers on StreamVid, though that was only one of her social media profiles. I was lucky if my StreamVid posts got a couple hundred views; Della's most popular videos had views in the *billions*. She hosted live on StreamVid every weekday like clockwork for an hour at 11:00 a.m., and her fans and followers all around the world would tune in to give her monetary gifts in the form of digital flowers, coins, and star emojis. Out of all of her followers, out of every single gushing fan, every emoji-laden request for attention, Della chose to chat regularly with me. Della understood me. Della was my *friend*.

For the last year, Della and I chatted online almost every single day, sharing life updates and just getting to know one another. I first found Della the way most everyone did, by scrolling through an endless array of videos on StreamVid. I was standing behind the register at Pet Planet on a dull and dreary Wednesday morning, hiding my phone from view when her brightly colored video caught my eye. I wasn't supposed to use my phone on the clock, but there was nothing to do, and I wanted to drown out the din of the chirping parakeets and screeching hamster wheels for a little while.

Della's post that day was a beautifully produced, thirty-second makeup tutorial featuring an amazing transformation that turned the lower half of her face into a skull. I gasped as I replayed the video and watched it over and over again, marveling at the magical artistry of cream makeup and brushwork against skin. I followed her immediately and was pleasantly surprised to get a follow back.

At the time, Della had around 50K followers — still an impressive number — yet she took the time to respond to little old *me*.

I still had a screenshot of our very first exchange saved in a folder on my phone.

AnimalLvr2002: This looks amazing!
DellaOfficial: Thanks, babe ;)

Feel-good chemicals flooded my brain at that first notification, and that was all it took; from then on, I was hooked on Della's content. I joined her official patrons-only fan-club page for ten dollars a month and waited patiently every Saturday for her exclusive content. I bought digital tokens to send to her at every live-streaming event to ensure that I retained a badge as one of her top fans and, of course, bought all of her merchandise (coffee mugs, keychain, hoodie, stickers). At least two or three times a week she would message me on her private, fans-only server and ask about my hobbies and interests. On my birthday, I even bought a two-minute shout-out video for myself from her, pretending to be one of my friends. That sounded pathetic, I knew, but even if I did have friends IRL, I couldn't tell them about my fixation on Della. Most people just didn't understand. Della was cool and beautiful and artistic. Everything I wanted to be. Everything I was not.

At the time, I knew I was spending too much time watching Della's content, but I couldn't help it. She kept me company and gave me hope. Her StreamVid page was the first thing I checked in the morning, and the last thing I watched before I went to sleep. She was always doing something new, something way ahead of the trends. Della's viral videos usually featured her doing some new dance craze that everyone would copy. I responded to her most popular dance video with a series of emojis (heart eyes, dancing woman, star, star, star), and more feel-good chemicals spiked in my veins. As one of her top fans, my comment was posted front and center above all of the other comments. I held my breath and waited for her to see my support and comment back.

"Casey, I need you to get your laundry out of the dryer."

My mother poked her head into my bedroom, the light from the hallway piercing my eyes. It was ten a.m. on a weekday, and I was still in bed watching videos, where I usually remained hidden under a pile of blankets until it was time for my shift at Pet Planet.

"Okay."

"Are you going to go down to the college today and talk to the advisor?"

"No time." I yawned. "I have to be at work in an hour."

"*Casey*, you said you would go today." My mother frowned at me from my open door, her eyes narrowed into disappointed slits.

"I'll go tomorrow," I lied.

"You're *nineteen*. It's not good for you to just sit in a dark room all day..."

"I know how old I am," I grumbled, and stood up. "Besides, I still don't know if college is for me."

"Oh really? You're satisfied with working at the pet store your entire life?"

"No. I just don't know what I want to do yet."

"That's fine, but you'll have to start paying rent soon. You've had a whole year after high school to figure out what you want to do with yourself."

"I know." I pushed past my mother into the hallway, hoping she would end her lecture. "I'll take care of it."

"Wait." She placed a hand on my shoulder, her eyes narrowing into critical slits. "Oh, *Casey*. Did you cut your own hair again?"

"It's just bangs," I said, raising a hand to my forehead.

"Well, if you dye it again, please put down some plastic or newspaper. Last time you got green hair dye all over the sink."

"Okay. Can I go get my laundry now?"

"Yes. Oh, and don't forget to change the lint trap!"

I sighed and padded down the carpeted hallway, avoiding the smiling gazes of my dearly departed grandparents, my parents, in their sepia-toned wedding photo, and my older siblings, in their high school graduation portraits. The hallway was a shrine to my family composed of thirty years of curated, dusty memories preserved behind glass picture frames that never

CHAPTER ONE

quite hung right. My own image smiled down at me in collage form, starting with my gap-toothed kindergarten photo and ending at my unsmiling senior portrait. I hadn't changed much since that picture was taken over a year ago.

As the youngest of five children and the only one still living at home, I got all of my mother's attention, whether I wanted it or not. My sisters and brother scattered in different directions after high school for college or job opportunities. Dad's business kept him at the office sixty hours a week, so it was just me and my mother a lot of the time. I know Mom meant well, but she still got on my nerves and was always in my business. My siblings were lucky or smart, or maybe just more motivated than me. They'd made their own way. They'd gotten out. I knew that I could, too, but I was frozen in place: trapped in my dusty old house, just like my grandparents' long-ago photographed smiles.

I loaded a pile of my jeans, T-shirts, socks, and underwear into a laundry basket, cleaned the lint trap, and turned back to my bedroom, as I'd done so many times before, and shuffled down the hall, already knowing exactly how the rest of my day would go. I would take a shower, get dressed in my Pet Planet uniform, work for eight hours, come home in the dark, eat whatever leftovers my mom had saved for dinner, and then stream Della videos until I fell asleep. Then I would do it all over again the next day, and then the next. Every day was boring and bland and exactly the same.

There were a few bright spots in my life though. My bearded dragon — Spike — was one of those things. I normally didn't like to own caged animals, since I felt so caged in all the time myself, but Spike needed a home after being bullied by another beardie at the pet store. Poor guy had one of his hind feet chewed off. My manager was going to euthanize Spike, but I begged them to let me take him home. Working in a pet store is tough sometimes. My heart was too tender, and the thought of putting Spike down just because he was missing a foot nearly sent me spiraling. I was glad I was able to save him though; besides Della, Spike was one of my only friends.

Marco was another bright spot in my day. We weren't exactly friends, but we weren't strangers either. Marco used to be a cashier at the pet store before he quit to work for the coffee shop in the mini mall across the way. He trained me on my first day, and even though I would deny it to anyone who asked, I had a little bit of a crush on him. He was cool, and he had long hair and a tattoo on his neck of a skull with diamonds for eyes. I treated myself to a fancy coffee a couple of times a week when I saw his van parked in the employee back lot. I didn't even really like coffee, but I did like talking to Marco. Did that make me a stalker? I hoped not.

After a quick shower, I pulled on my jeans and butter-yellow Pet Planet polo shirt while they were still somewhat warm from the dryer, the toasty clothes encasing my body like a hug. I fed Spike and gave him some attention, my gaze flicking to the phone on my bed as I stroked his scaly body. I was trying to get better about not checking my phone so much for notifications, but so far, I was failing. When I was little, my oldest sister had a phone that she called her "Crackberry" because she was so hooked on it. That was me and my phone now. Addicted.

I put Spike back in his cage, washed my hands, and checked my phone before leaving for work. Still no response from Della. If I was lucky, the pet store would be slow again and I could leave my phone running during her eleven a.m. live stream. Maybe she would respond to my posts then.

I waved goodbye to my mother, grabbed my backpack and

CHAPTER ONE

keys, and headed out the door to my beige Buick LeSabre waiting in the driveway. The car was about as old as I was, but it was free, the only inheritance I'd gotten from my grandfather on my dad's side. Grandpa Don had kept the car in good shape at least, and it had low miles from him only driving to the bowling alley and the grocery store. I didn't even know what kind of car I would have bought anyway if I'd had a choice. There were a lot of things I still didn't know about myself.

My heart sank as I pulled into the parking lot at work later that morning and saw no sign of Marco's van. Perhaps it was for the best. I checked my reflection in the visor mirror of the car and tugged at my freshly cut bangs. Faded green dye clung to the ends of my shoulder-length bottle-bleached hair, and I mused for a minute about what color to pick next. Blue and pink were so overdone. Maybe purple next time.

Reagan, the store manager, glanced up from behind the register and waved me over as I walked through the Pet Planet automatic sliding doors. A half dozen customers milled about the store, examining dog toys, picking up kitty treats, and cooing at the parakeets and hamsters. A huge pallet of canned dog food stood at the end of aisle three waiting to be stocked. I cringed as Reagan's gaze flitted from me to the tower of unpacked boxes.

"Hey, Casey. Sean called out today. I need you to stock the shelves."

"But I'm supposed to be at the register," I said, glancing down at Reagan's open paperback. I wasn't the only one who enjoyed leisure time on the clock.

"I need to run the register today. I'm putting you on the floor to stock instead."

"Fine." I turned, rolled my eyes, and walked toward the break room. Typical. I would have to just listen to Della's live stream instead of watching it. I stashed my backpack in my locker, clocked in, popped in my earbuds, and opened up the StreamVid app as I made my way back out to the floor. My chest flooded with warmth as Della's big eyes and gleaming smile greeted me from the glass screen. Today she was dressed like a living windup doll, her cheeks painted red and hair done up like a yarn wig. I pouted and shoved the phone into my back pocket. I hated to miss any of Della's live streams.

That day, I cut open cardboard boxes, stacked rows and rows of canned dog foods, and wiped down dusty shelves to the tune of Della's sweet voice in my ear. Della made work more enjoyable. Della made me want to be a better version of myself. Della made me want more out of life. Della. Della. *Della*.

Chapter Two

Do you know that camera trick used in movies where it looks like the hallway never ends? Or where the walls seem to be closing in? Those dreams where you feel like something you can't see is chasing you? This was how it felt in my everyday life before Della.

Without her positive messages to give me a boost, my insomnia and anxiety became even worse. For whatever reason, Della didn't respond to the comments I posted that day before work, or the next day, or the day after that. Her radio silence made me feel like I was falling. My chest hurt like something heavy was lying on it, and no matter what I did, I couldn't take in a whole, deep breath.

I did everything that I could think of to get Della's attention. I bought her newest line of perfume from her website, even though I didn't wear perfume. I posted a StreamVid review of her products that I already owned and told my viewers where to get them and tagged her. She kept posting videos, which could have been prescheduled, but her live streams went dark, and I feared the worst. Either something was wrong with Della or she no longer wanted to communicate with me, and both of those possibilities made me feel like dying.

On Thursday, I went to the community college and met with a

student advisor under a mental and emotional fog of my own creation. The advisor was a woman near my mother's age with kind eyes. She asked me what I was interested in, but I wasn't really there with her mentally. My mind was with Della. I remembered saying that I might want to work with animals, but I wasn't sure. The advisor signed me up for a few beginner courses to start in January anyway, because what else was I supposed to do? At least, for the time being, I would be enrolled in college to get my mother off my back until I could figure out what I really wanted to do. *Gotta keep moving forward, Casey. Can't hide in your room forever.*

By the time my Sunday shift at Pet Planet rolled around, I was in full panic mode about Della. My efforts at weaning myself from my phone were all but futile, as I began to check every fifteen minutes for some kind of reply or sign of life from my favorite streamer. Finally, some time in the afternoon as I slumped behind the register, my phone pinged a notification. Electric pops of adrenaline shot up and down my spine as I flicked to the StreamVid app to see her message waiting for me.

AnimalLvr2002: Hey Della! Just checking in to make sure you're okay. Haven't seen you post in a few days.

DellaOfficial: You're so sweet! Just between you and me, I've been sick. I was in the hospital, but I'm home now and doing so much better.

I clasped a hand to my chest as I read and reread her message over and over. Della wasn't ignoring me, and she wasn't dead. Relief washed over me as I frantically typed back my response.

AnimalLvr2002: Oh, I'm so glad to hear that! I'm sorry you're sick though.

"Hey, whatcha doing?"

CHAPTER TWO

I jumped and gasped as Sean leaned over the counter, his lips set in a smirk. Sean and I had gone to the same school but had run in different crowds back then. I thought he was kind of annoying with his perfect high-and-tight haircut and golden-retriever puppy-dog personality, but then again, I tended to think everyone was annoying.

"Jesus, Sean. You scared me half to death."

"If Reagan catches you on your phone, you're toast," he said, straightening up. "Not that she doesn't read all day behind the register."

"Right?" I chuckled, avoiding direct eye contact. "Did you need something?"

He snapped his gum and pointed to the go-backs basket behind the register. "I just came to see if you had anything that needed to be reshelved."

"If Reagan catches you chewing gum on the floor, you're toast." I smirked back and turned to grab the basket.

"You want some gum?" Sean reached down into the pocket of his khaki pants.

"Are you saying I have bad breath?" I handed him the go-backs basket filled with unwanted fish food, cat treats, and a dog sweater.

"Har har." He took the basket and passed me a warm stick of gum wrapped in silver paper. For a moment, I considered the fact that the gum was so warm because of his body heat, and all of the blood in my body rushed to my cheeks.

"I, uh, I heard you had to stock for me the other day when I called out," Sean said, scratching the back of his neck. "Sorry about that."

"It's okay." I popped the neon-green stick into my mouth. The minty gum was soft; it practically melted on my tongue.

"Anyway, thanks." Sean stared down at the basket and lingered for a moment. It seemed like he wanted to say something more, but what it was, I couldn't guess. Probably just wanted to see if I could cover another shift for him. I pursed my lips, my gaze darting from Sean's dark eyes and thick lashes back to my phone again. I desperately wanted to get back to my conversation with Della. Why of all times did Sean want to chat with me *now*?

"How's Spike doing?"

"Oh." I blinked and nodded. "He's doing really well. Eating a lot, seems pretty happy."

"I'm glad to hear that. I would have taken him myself when I found out he was going to get put down, but my mom doesn't like caged animals in the house."

"Yeah. I get it," I said, glancing at my phone again.

"Well, I should probably put this stuff back on the shelves," he said. "Thanks again."

"No prob." I bit my lip and waited as Sean gave a weird sort of wave-salute goodbye. My heart raced as I picked up my phone and checked the message.

DellaOfficial: You're so sweet to check on me! I haven't told the rest of my followers yet, but since you are my #1 supporter, I suppose I can tell you first. I've been diagnosed with a very rare form of cancer. Actually, I don't know how much longer I'll be able to post on StreamVid.

Cancer. My stomach dropped to my feet as I read and reread her message. The idea of Della hurting or being in pain drove a knife of dread into my heart. I didn't know what disturbed me more: Della being ill with a potentially life-threatening disease, or the possibility that she might have to stop streaming. Still, the fact that she'd confided in me and only me with this very personal, very life-changing information made me feel special. Della really *was* my friend. I knew it.

AnimalLvr2002: I'm so sorry! Let me know how I can help.

"Excuse me, miss. How much for this leash?"

I slipped my phone into my back pocket as a grandmotherly woman held out a leash to me. I smiled and scanned it.

"It's twelve ninety-nine. Did you want to buy it?"

The woman nodded, so I bagged her leash and took her payment. Through the entire transaction, all I could think of was Della lying in a hospital bed, hooked up to wires, her beautiful, doll-like features sunken and gray. This was awful news. Horrible. The worst. I handed the woman her change, the receipt, and her bag, my head still in the clouds.

"Have a nice Della... I mean, nice day."

"You too, dear."

I watched the older woman leave, my heart clenched tight as a fist. I knew that Della would need all of the love and support she could get. As her number one fan and friend, it was up to me to help somehow.

I hid my phone behind the register and watched as Della made a tearful announcement on her daily eleven a.m. live stream. She was dressed very simply in all black with her hair done up in a black turban against a black background. Her pale, wide-eyed gaze stared back at me like a floating, disembodied head as she read her statement.

"Hi, fans and friends, it's me, Della. I just wanted to drop in and say that you'll probably be seeing me around here less and less because I received some very bad news about my health. I'll be in and out of hospitals for treatment soon, so if you don't see me here on StreamVid then that's why. Thank you so much for all of your support. I love you all."

Della blew a kiss to the camera, and her live stream ended.

I sighed and shook my head in disbelief. No more makeup tutorials. No more positive inspirational mantras. No more silly songs or dances. No more Della. *No.* It couldn't be.

For the rest of my shift, I racked my brain trying to think of how I could help or what could be done. I didn't know her financial situation, but my guess was that she, like most full-time creators, probably didn't have good insurance. Cancer treatments were lengthy and expensive, and even though she was probably making good money as a streamer, Della would likely need all the help and support she could get.

Reagan relieved me for my lunch break around noon, and I walked over to the café, as I often did when Marco's van was in the parking lot. Back when I'd first started working at Pet Planet, Marco had told me that he had a motorcycle but, after a particularly bad accident, had decided not to get back on the bike again. I and everyone else at Pet Planet had donated to his FundFairy account while he was recovering. The memory sparked an idea that I couldn't get away from as I entered the café: I was going to start a FundFairy campaign for Della.

The scent of air-conditioning and fresh coffee beans greeted me as I entered the café, smooth jazz floating through the speakers. Marco leaned behind the counter, tall and lanky and cool as ever. He offered a slight smile of recognition as I approached, and my breath hitched in my throat.

"Oh, hey, Carrie."

"Hey." Panic fluttered in my chest. Marco had never learned my real name, and he had been calling me Carrie for so long, I didn't have it in me to tell him.

"Hazelnut latte?"

"No, not today. I, um, I had a question, actually." I cleared

CHAPTER TWO

my throat. "You know when everyone at the pet store did the FundFairy thing for you after your accident? I was wondering how that worked."

"Oh, I dunno." Marco tucked a strand of long dark hair behind his ear. His nails were painted black, and he had a new tattoo on his knuckles: his name in a thick black gothic type. "They just, like, took my address, and then I eventually got a check in the mail."

"Cool. Cool." I nodded.

"Why, are you sick or somethin'?" Marco coughed, took out his phone, and began to scroll.

"No. I was just thinking of setting something up," I said, my voice warbling. "Like, a fundraiser for animals."

"Oh, right. 'Cause you like animals so much," he said, his eyes flicking from me to his screen again. "That would be cool."

"Yeah. Cool." I sucked in a long, slow breath as he continued to scroll on his phone. "Well, thanks. I gotta get back."

"Yep. See ya."

"See ya."

My face burned as I left the café and headed back toward Pet Planet. Why did I bother with Marco? He didn't even know my name. He was very pretty though. *Too* pretty. Ugh.

I hurried past Reagan on my way to the break room as she flipped through her latest paperback behind the register. I usually preferred to spend my lunch break at a restaurant, but I was making an effort to be more responsible with money. I'd actually packed a lunch that day, so I was feeling somewhat proud of myself despite the Della-induced haze I was in.

I sat in the small break room and munched on my peanut-butter sandwich as I started up a FundFairy account for Della on my phone. But when I got to the end of the application, it asked for the address of the recipient, and I froze. I couldn't use my address; that felt wrong. Della should get all of the money. Only... would she give me her real address?

AnimalLvr2002: Hey Della! I had the idea to set up a FundFairy account for you to help with your medical expenses. I'm going to start posting soon on StreamVid, but it's asking for an address to send the funds to.

I took another bite of my sandwich, but before I could even swallow, the ellipses underneath my message flashed to indicate that she was typing. My pulse ratcheted up as her response lit up on my screen.

DellaOfficial: You're the best! My address needs to remain confidential though, okay? I wouldn't give this info out if you weren't my #1 fan. You can direct the payments to 205 Orange Avenue, Tampa, Florida, 33609. Thanks babe!

My lower lip hung open as I read and reread the message. Della's actual address.

AnimalLvr2002: Thank you! I'll start posting the FundFairy information soon. Feel better!

My heart was pounding in my neck. *Florida.* Of course she would live in such a bright, cheerful place. The weather was probably beautiful there right now; the sky outside the pet store was bleak and gray, with winter's end nowhere in sight. I flipped to the navigation app on my phone and typed it in. Twelve hours away. Tampa was a long drive, but I could make it in a day if I wanted to.

Florida. Della. Cancer. The cocktail of heady thoughts floated in my brain the rest of the day and into the night as I planned my StreamVid posts to support her health journey. Della would see that I was her most devoted, most caring fan. I would do a good thing to help her, since Della was always there to help

CHAPTER TWO

us. Della would be well again, and at the end of it all, she would have one person and one person alone to thank for it.

Me.

Chapter Three

When I was a little girl, I would cry myself to sleep thinking of all of the kittens in the world that didn't have a home. I would imagine them mewling, wretched and hungry without their mother to care for them. Horrible scenarios would invade my thoughts with all of the graphic things that I heard adults did to unwanted kittens and puppies. I felt helpless knowing that there was nothing I could do to help every single lost or abandoned baby animal in the world. I was a tenderhearted little kid from the get-go, and always had a soft spot for helpless creatures. Animals were so much better than people for the most part. Animals never scared me. It was humans who were usually the dangerous ones.

Those same anxieties and feelings of helplessness returned when it came to dealing with the reality of Della's illness. I hated that I was so far removed from her. I wanted to *help*. However, unlike when I was a kid and felt like I couldn't do anything, now I had a way to actually make a difference.

Over the next week, I posted on StreamVid multiple times a day promoting Della's FundFairy account, encouraging other members of "Della Nation," as she called her fans, to pitch in and donate. I watched with glee as her fund grew and grew, and

CHAPTER THREE

with it, my own StreamVid subscribers grew as well. I got brave and began to post videos of Spike doing cute bearded-dragon things, but mostly, I talked about how we as a community could help Della in her time of need.

Della's StreamVid account went dark again almost as soon as I began her FundFairy campaign, but I tried my best to remain calm. I knew she was likely getting treatment or simply resting, but I didn't like the feeling of the unknown. I messaged her to let her know that her FundFairy account was doing well, but got no response. No matter what I did to try and distract myself, I always found my thoughts returning to Della. When it came to her health, I feared the worst, but still tried to keep hope.

I knew that I shouldn't, but after almost a week of no contact, I looked up Della's address again. The internet search quickly produced an image of her home from an old real estate listing. Della lived in a nice little suburban neighborhood, though that fact didn't surprise me too much. The exterior of her modest, modern home was perfectly manicured and lined with leafy green palm trees, waxy yellow and green bushes, and hibiscus plants with vibrant red blossoms. There was a wide picture window and a paved brick path leading to fancy double front doors with a wreath that said *HOME*. It occurred to me that perhaps Della still lived with her parents like I did. It made sense.

"Casey, do you need anything for school?"

Mom sat down on the edge of my bed as I was editing yet another StreamVid post. College classes were set to start the following month, and I should have been excited or at the very least nervous. I had been so wrapped up in my Della campaign that I'd honestly forgotten.

"Oh. I think I need to get books. Probably some notebooks. I think I need to pay for a parking pass too."

"Well, just let me and Dad know. Money is tight, but it always is. We'll help you pay for your books if you need help." Mom leaned over and kissed me on top of my head. "Whatcha working on?"

"Oh, just a fundraiser for my friend. She's sick, and I'm heading up a FundFairy for her," I said, turning the computer to face her. "Her followers have already donated about twenty thousand dollars."

"Casey!" My mother slipped her reading glasses from the top of her head onto the bridge of her nose. "This is wonderful! I didn't know you had a friend who was sick, though."

"Yeah, it's awful. She's so creative and nice. I hate that she's going through this," I said.

"You know what? You should bring her flowers," Mom said, patting me on the knee. "That would be a nice gesture."

"She's not that kind of friend." I paused and chewed on the thought. "I mean, she doesn't exactly live nearby."

"It's just a suggestion. When my friend Kathy was in the hospital, no one visited her except for me." Mom huffed and held up her hands. "Her husband even left her. It's awful. Women spend their entire lives taking care of their families, but then they get sick and it's crickets."

"That's terrible," I said.

"Anyway, I'm proud of you for having the initiative to help. And for starting school." Mom nodded. "Are you working today?"

"No. I'm off for the next three days," I said, the gears in my brain turning.

"Well, I'm headed to the grocery store soon." She stood up and walked toward the door. "Holler if you need me to pick up anything."

Take flowers to Della. Why not? I had three whole days off in a row and nothing really to do. My gaze flicked to Spike in his terrarium. He was perched on his favorite stick, soaking up some light. I couldn't leave him. Mom thought he was gross; she wouldn't want to take care of him while I was gone. I had a little money saved up, so gas and hotels would be covered. All I needed was for someone to take care of Spike, and I knew exactly whom to ask.

Pet Planet had a messaging server that the staff used to communicate with each other. If someone needed to cover another person's shift or if there was some kind of news that we all needed to know, then we would just post it there. Sean, as usual, was online when I went into the server room. I pressed his cheesy, goofy smiling avatar and began to type.

Casey: Hey, u busy

Sean: No whats up

Casey: Can you watch Spike for a couple of days? I need to go out of town.

Sean: Sure. I'm working this morning. You can just bring him to the store.

Casey: Ah, thanks man. I owe u

I finished editing the StreamVid clip and closed my laptop as a surge of adrenaline rushed through me. Visit Della. Why not? It was like my mom said: we should support our friends. Maybe a friendly face was exactly what Della needed. Even if it didn't work out, I could treat myself to a stay at the beach just once before the drudgery of college began. I didn't have anything else going on. What was the worst that could happen?

I packed an overnight bag and waited for Mom to leave before grabbing Spike's travel cage and food and heading out the door.

Twelve hours was a long drive, but I could make it. It was early, and if I got moving, I could be in Tampa well before midnight. I had never driven that far before, and I only had two hundred bucks and a nearly maxed-out credit card to my name. If I let myself worry or thought about it too much, I would chicken out and not go.

"Okay, Spike," I said, securing his travel cage with a seatbelt in the back seat of my car. "You're going on a little vacation, too."

* * *

Sean met me in the parking lot at Pet Planet later that morning as anxious pools of sweat began to blossom under my arms. My pulse ratcheted up as he approached my car with a mile-wide smile, his hair sticking up at comical angles. I tugged at the hem of my T-shirt and wished for a split second that I had bothered to dress a little nicer that day.

"Nice car." Sean nodded, his smile morphing into a smirk. "For a grandpa."

"Haha. Very funny," I said, unbuckling the travel crate. "Well, joke's on you, because this was actually my grandfather's car. I inherited it after he died."

"My bad." He grimaced.

"It's fine," I said, with a half-hearted chuckle. "Here. Thanks again for watching him."

He took the travel crate from me and smiled at Spike. "Hey, buddy."

"I feel better leaving him with you. Feeding him grosses my mom out," I said. "I owe you."

"Nah. You've had to cover for me before. We're even. Besides,

I like Spike." Sean made a goofy face at the reptile. It almost looked like Spike smiled back. "I'm happy to do it."

"He needs to eat three times a day. I packed a couple of days of fresh bugs, but if he runs out you can get more here."

"Cool."

"I'll pick him up on my next shift if that's okay," I said.

"Fine. Where are you going? If you don't mind me asking."

I paused, not sure what to say. I hadn't even told my parents where I was going. No one really knew the extent of my friendship with Della, and Sean was nice, but he probably wouldn't get it.

"I'm going to Tampa. To see a friend."

"Florida. Cool, cool. The weather is probably better there right now," he said.

"Definitely."

"Well, have a good time," Sean said, his lips curling into a strange sort of smile. "Maybe when you get back, we could, like, go for a coffee or something like that."

"Coffee?"

"Yeah, you're always going over to that café," Sean said, scratching the bridge of his nose. "I was just thinking, maybe I could buy you a coffee sometime."

"Uh, yeah," I said, taken aback. "Sure."

"Cool."

"Cool." I tugged at my bangs. They needed a trim again. "Well, I guess I'll see you when I get back."

"Yep. Have fun."

The sheer mention of coffee made me yawn and reminded me that I had a long trip ahead. If I was going to go all the way to Florida to deliver a bouquet of flowers to Della, I definitely deserved a hazelnut latte first, and it was just my luck that a certain beat-up old van was parked in the employee lot.

The café was busier than usual as I stood in line and waited for Marco to serve me. His long dark hair was piled on top of his head in a bun, and the dark scruff on his upper lip was growing into a thick mustache. My heart skipped a beat as he glanced at me with a familiar, friendly nod.

"Yo, Carrie. What's up?"

"Actually, it's Casey," I said, and cleared my throat. "I should have told you that a long time ago. My name is actually Casey."

"Oh. My bad. You want a hazelnut latte, Casey?"

I scoffed as Marco held the thick black marker to the disposable cup made of recycled, one-hundred-percent compostable material. I was on my way to see Della, someone who actually knew my name and cared about me. Fuck this guy. "You know, I think I'll just have a chai tea today."

"Right on." Marco turned and steamed the milk and chai, then handed me the cup of piping-hot tea. "That's two seventy-nine."

I reached into my bag, grabbed my wallet, pulled out a five-dollar bill, and slid it across the counter. "Keep the change."

"Cool."

"Thanks," I said, the chai warming my hands. "See ya."

"See ya."

I smiled to myself as I left the café, leaving my dusty old house, Pet World, school, and even Marco behind me. I was lighter. Freer than ever before. I had three whole days ahead of me with endless possibilities. I wasn't just going to hide in my bedroom anymore waiting for life to happen to me. I slid behind the wheel of my car, cranked my grandfather's old stereo, and set my navigation app to Tampa, Florida.

Chapter Four

When I was little, Magic World was my favorite place to go, and I dreamed of living there amongst the facade of castles and brightly colored roller coaster rides. Florida was so bright and warm and green everywhere you looked; the sky was always blue and the sun was always shining. My hometown was cold and bleak, with a gray winter sky and a landscape that was less than inspiring. In comparison, escaping to Florida on my own felt as new and magical to me as my friendship with Della.

The interstate winding through central Georgia and northern Florida was long and boring and monotonous, but my senses were on full alert for the first time in ages, and I finally felt excited about something. I had made the drive a few times before in the back seat of my parents' SUV for trips to Orlando, but never on my own. I stopped along the way twice to refuel and take bathroom breaks, loading up on gas-station hot dogs, soda, candy, and chips. Grandpa Don's old Buick got pretty good gas mileage and offered a fast, smooth ride. I listened to podcasts from my favorite animal experts along the way, as well as a few tutorials on what to expect in veterinary school. It would require a lot of work, and an expensive education, but the more I thought about it, the more I realized that I really did want to make animal care my focus. If only I could get my attention away from my online life long enough to buckle down and just do it.

Driving on the interstate made obsessively checking my phone impossible, and it occurred to me that this was the first stretch of time in a while where my phone wasn't always in my hand. After I had driven a hundred miles or so, I stopped at a rest station and texted my mother to tell her that I was taking her advice to visit my sick friend, and then I put her on silent. I knew that Dad wouldn't care, but Mom would be pissed that I'd left without saying goodbye in person.

The sun dipped low above the horizon as the Florida state line appeared, and my heart fluttered in my chest. My legs were stiff and my shoulders and back hurt, but the promise of reaching my destination reenergized me. I sipped on a giant sixty-four-ounce soda as the miles flew by under my tires and the exits for Tampa came into sight.

I had already blown almost half of my budget on gas as I rolled into town, and I realized that my initial plan to stay at the beach wasn't going to work. All of the beach hotels were too far away from Della's place and far too expensive or booked up, so I checked into a roadside motel instead. For $67.89 I got a bed, a bathroom, a television, air-conditioning, and a door that locked. That was all I needed.

It was near midnight when I finally settled into my motel room and collapsed on the bed, exhausted from the drive. Mom was surprisingly gentle over text, telling me to be safe and to call her if I needed anything. I guessed signing up for college classes really had gotten her off my back. I texted her back to let her know that I was okay, the name of the motel I was staying at, and that I loved her. I also texted Sean and was happy when he replied with a series of selfies of him mugging for the camera with Spike.

After a full day of keeping my phone at a safe distance, I allowed myself to indulge in a social media binge. I checked Della's FundFairy account first, astonished to find that the balance had reached nearly twenty-five thousand dollars from her supporters, officially a quarter of the way to the one-hundred-thousand-dollar goal. I made a quick update video and fell asleep on top of the scratchy motel bedspread, scrolling through StreamVid and the responses to my videos on Della.

* * *

The following morning burned bright and hopeful as I stepped out of my motel room into the dizzyingly bright Florida sunlight. It was as though the volume had been turned up on everything; the air was lighter, the world was more vivid and crisp. The day was full of possibilities. I didn't have much of a plan for what I was going to do when I met Della, only to bring her flowers and hope that I wasn't intruding. I'd tried to contact her so many times, and I knew that technically it wasn't cool to just show up uninvited and unannounced, but I reasoned that Della wouldn't mind. We were friends.

I dressed as nicely as I knew how that day, in a plain black dress, tights, and my high-top sneakers. I even did my eye makeup the way Della had done in one of her StreamVid tutorials, creating a dramatic look with thick winged liner. Then I went to the nearest grocery store and picked out the best bouquet of roses they had before my stomach began to rumble. Food. I needed a little something to eat before meeting my idol/friend IRL.

I picked up a breakfast sandwich and two hazelnut lattes from the nearest coffee shop (hazelnut was Della's favorite, too) and sat in the parking lot, practicing what I would say. What if Della wasn't home? What if she was admitted to a hospital somewhere? Or, worse, what if she didn't want to see me?

Either way, if my visit didn't work out, I could leave the flowers and coffee at the door and spend the rest of the day at the beach sans tights and sneakers. I finished my breakfast, set the navigation app to Della's address, and pulled out of the parking lot fueled by eggs, caffeine, and adrenaline.

It was just after eight a.m. when I pulled into Della's tree-lined suburban neighborhood. Her house was situated in the middle of a pristine development with nicely maintained sidewalks, street signs, and neighborhood-watch warnings. Basketball hoops, bikes, and tree swings littered the front yards of the homes, signaling squarely middle-class families and the occasional retiree. Finally, I reached 205 Orange Avenue and the exterior of Della's home came into view.

The property didn't look exactly like it had on the real estate listing, but it was close enough. The house must have been newer at the time the photo had been taken, as now the exterior seemed worn and faded. The grass was overgrown in some parts and patchy in others, the once meticulously cared-for flower beds full of weeds. Just like Della, the house seemed sick. In need of care.

A white minivan was parked in the driveway of the house, and just as I was getting out of my car, the garage door opened. A teenage boy with dark hair burst from inside the garage, which from my vantage point seemed overstuffed with cardboard boxes, trash bags, and all manner of junk. A younger girl emerged from the garage, and she and the boy both got into the minivan as a sour-faced woman with short blond hair and sunglasses followed them. I hunched down behind the wheel of my car and watched as they loaded into the van.

That must be Della's mom and siblings.

I continued my stakeout hidden from view as the van rumbled to life, backed out of the driveway on screeching wheels, and disappeared in the opposite direction. I exhaled, my heart pounding in my neck like a techno beat as I considered my next move. Should I knock on the door? If Della was inside resting, I wouldn't want to disturb her. My hand trembled as I reached for my phone and flipped to StreamVid to check her profile. To my surprise, Della had posted an announcement only a few moments before that she would be resuming her daily streaming series that day to give an update on her diagnosis. I clutched the phone to my chest, relieved. Della was feeling well enough to be on camera again. Perhaps she would answer the door for me after all.

I checked my makeup in the mirror one last time and brushed a few stray crumbs from breakfast off my dress before stepping out of the car. I had never done anything like this in my life, and I wasn't entirely sure what to say, or how to even explain why I was there. The fact was, I wanted to be Della's friend in real life and not just online. I'd had a few friends here and there when I was in school, but never a *best* friend. I'd traveled all this way, and here at the final moment, I didn't want to freeze or screw anything up. I needed to see Della in person just once to let her know how much her friendship meant to me. How much *she* meant to me.

With the bouquet in one hand and the latte in the other, I crossed the road to Della's house. My head felt as though it was trying to detach from my neck as I neared her front door, my vision blurring. I was forgetting to breathe. I stood on her front stoop, closed my eyes, and took a slow, centering breath. I opened my eyes, still dizzy, and pushed the doorbell with my heart in my throat.

I recoiled as the bark from a large-breed dog immediately sounded on the other side of the double doors. I waited on Della's front stoop, hoping her dog didn't know how to chew through doors. I stood there for what felt like an eternity staring at the faded *HOME* wreath as the sound of scraping nails and a vicious bark warned me from the other side of the door.

I was considering ringing the doorbell again when the crunch of tires against gravel caught my attention. I turned my head to see the white minivan pulling up into the driveway and made eye contact with the woman in the driver's seat. I managed a smile and waved with the bouquet in my hand. She glared back at me, clenching the wheel, and as she got out of the van, I began to feel like the whole thing was a mistake.

Oh no. This isn't a good time. I'm not wanted. I should have never come...

"Can I help you?" The woman walked around the front of the van with her lips set in a thin, annoyed-looking line. She was dressed like every other suburban mom I had ever met: in sneakers, a pair of black yoga pants, and a short-sleeved tee. Her salon-highlighted hair was perfectly coiffed in a chin-length bob, her dark eyes piercing and full of questions. The closer the woman got, the more apparent it was that she was related to Della.

"Hi. I'm so sorry to bother you. I'm a friend of Della's. I just wanted to visit and bring her flowers. I hope this isn't a bad time."

The woman's features softened, but her body language became more rigid as she approached me. I was terrible at guessing ages, but I figured that she was probably in her forties? If she was Della's mom, she would have to be that old at least. Her gaze trailed up and down my form, landing on the coffee and flowers. She crossed her arms and cleared her throat.

"Della is sick. She can't see anyone right now."

"I know! I'm so sorry. I just wanted to bring her these to cheer her up." I extended the flowers and coffee in her direction. "I came all this way. Can you just tell her I'm here? Please?"

The woman licked her lips and accepted the flowers and coffee. She brought the bouquet to her nose, closed her eyes, and inhaled their fragrance.

"What's your name?"

"Casey," I said. "I'm one of Della's biggest fans."

"Casey, huh." She sniffed the coffee and chuckled to herself before meeting my gaze with a smile. "Would you like to come in?"

Chapter Five

When I was in the second grade, I went to a friend's house to play for the day. She lived on the "bad" side of town, which I didn't really understand at the time. Now that I was older I knew that kind of thinking was bullshit. Looking back, I was surprised my overly protective mother let me go to her house in the first place. I had grown up thinking my family was poor, but seeing the way my friend lived made me realize that we weren't poor at all. This friend — Ashley was her name, I think? — had a lot of siblings, like I did, only they all shared one room. Six kids, three bunk beds, and three dressers all crammed into one room amongst a pile of toys, trash, and clothes. This was how Della's house looked, only bigger.

"Don't mind Hercules, he's just a big baby," Della's mother said. She placed the coffee and flowers on a side table and grabbed the large black-and-brown dog by the scruff as I eased my way into the living room. The dog was enormous — he must have weighed a hundred pounds at least — and seemed to be some kind of mixed-breed rottweiler. The dog did not seem to like my presence there at all and continued a stream of ferocious-sounding barks as she put him into a room and closed the door. She turned to me, wiped her hands on her yoga pants, and smiled.

CHAPTER FIVE

"Can I get you anything to drink, Casey?"

"Just water would be nice." I glanced around the house, breathing in the stale animal-and-dust-scented air.

"I'll be right back."

I hugged myself and took in the contents of the crowded living room as I waited. There wasn't anywhere to sit in the overly cluttered house, save for a sectional sofa underneath a mountain of boxes and laundry baskets. The walls were painted a sickly salmon pink in a flat paint that showed every handprint, scuff mark, and dog-nose smudge. Veils of dusty cobweb trailed from the corner of the ceiling to a fabric valance along the front window, each gossamer strand shuddering against the piped-in air-conditioning. I blinked as something akin to shock seeped into my bones. The idea of my fabulous, beautiful, perfect friend Della having to live in a place like this made me uncomfortable.

"Here you are." Her mother returned with a glass of water in an old, well-worn tumbler from Magic World.

I skeptically accepted the glass. "Thanks."

"Della is having a hard time with her treatments," she explained. "She's been sleeping a lot, so I don't know if she'll be up to seeing visitors today."

"I'm so sorry," I said. "I shouldn't have come without being invited, but I wanted to check and see if she's okay."

"Are you the friend who set up the FundFairy account for her?"

"Mm-hmm." I nodded, taking a sip of the water. So Della *had* mentioned me. Maybe my presence here wasn't so awkward after all. "It's actually a quarter of the way funded already."

"That's so kind of you." Her eyes sparkled, and she sucked in a short, sharp breath. "Would you like to go look at her studio?"

"Really?" I said, my voice high and tight. "I don't want to impose more than I already am."

"No! No imposition at all," she said. "Follow me."

Her mother turned and walked through the small living room to an area that at one point must have been the dining room. Like the sectional sofa, the table in the center of the room was stacked with piles of paperwork, plastic storage bins with dusty lids, toys, and other unidentifiable junk. An antique china cabinet dominated the far wall and was stocked full of figurines, decorative plates, and odds and ends. On top of the cabinet was an old framed family photo of a blond woman, a large man, and two small children.

"It's just this way." She opened up a glass sliding door partially obscured by a wall of cardboard boxes filled with newspapers and magazines. Something scampered inside one of the boxes as she nudged it with her foot, and I jumped at the noise. I normally wasn't the type to be judgy about the way people lived, but this house seemed beyond just normal clutter and everyday mess; everything about this house was toxic. Della's house was making me edgy, and I was very eager to get back out into the fresh air.

My stomach clenched as I followed the woman out onto the patio. Something didn't feel right. How could Della, or anyone else for that matter, possibly stand to live in these conditions? If she was sick, certainly all of the dust wasn't going to help in her recovery. She needed me to help her get out of here. Della deserved better than this.

The patio was equally as cluttered as the inside of the house and looked out onto a vast backyard and a half-full swimming pool that had turned green and murky. Stacks of lawn furniture and deflated, molding pool toys littered the once welcoming space. The patio had been uncared for long enough that weeds had bloomed through cracks in the concrete, their white and yellow flowers reaching for the sun. The metal cage that surrounded the in-ground pool had once been a grand addition to the house, but now nearly every rectangular screen panel was ripped and torn. A warm breeze blew across the yard, and the tattered black mesh strips that clung to the mildew-speckled frame danced on the wind.

I continued to follow her past a neglected vegetable garden toward the far corner of the property, where a large, windowless building loomed. The structure looked like the kind of double-wide shed someone could build on their own from the big-box hardware stores, the kind that some enterprising folks even knew how to turn into a tiny home. A sturdy-looking padlock on the front of the shed held the barn-style doors together, and the woman reached for it as she approached. She took a key ring from her pocket, undid the lock, and opened the door.

"This is where all the magic happens." She turned to me and smiled, motioning for me to enter. "Go on in."

She flicked on a light switch and revealed the contents of the converted shed. Unlike the house, this space was spotless, cozy, and expertly decorated to look like a miniature home studio. I immediately recognized one of the backdrops that Della frequently used in her videos on one side of the shed, and my excitement grew. At the other end of the room was a dressing table with a mirror, an LED ring light, and a makeup case. My pulse picked up speed as I recognized more props, costumes, and other items from Della's past streaming videos. It was real. I was really there in Della's studio.

"I can't believe it." I sighed. "This is really where she films all her live streams?"

"Yep." The woman nodded toward the vanity. "Go ahead. Have a seat."

"Really? Is that okay?"

"Sure. Della won't mind."

I willed my feet to move toward the vanity as something gnawed and clawed at the pit of my stomach. This visit wasn't turning out exactly as I had envisioned, but still, it was a dream to be in Della's studio, sitting at her vanity in the very same spot where she filmed every day. It was almost surreal to be on the reverse side of the camera, to be immersed in the mirror image of a space I knew so well. I had made this happen. I was here on the other side of the glass screen in a world that had seemed so untouchable to me before now. The realization was overwhelming.

I eased myself into the vanity chair and examined the contents of Della's extensive makeup collection. To my left was a rainbow palette of eyeshadows, a half dozen lipsticks, and a tube of mascara. To my right was a used bottle of liquid foundation and a ring light with a built-in phone stand. A roll of makeup brushes was laid out on the top of the vanity, waiting to be used. My head spun as I lifted one of the sleek brushes by its silver handle and examined the bristles. I blinked slowly, returned the brush to its sheath, and glanced at my reflection in the mirror. I looked odd. Pale. Behind my shoulder, Della's mother stood with her hands on her hips in a way that told me she was waiting for something. It was a stance my own mother took all the time.

"I'm sorry, do you think I could get some more water?" I said, reaching up to touch my throat. "I'm feeling very thirsty again."

"What do you think of the studio?" she asked.

"It's amazing." I closed my eyes and yawned. "Honestly, it's not what I expected."

"It never is."

I yawned again, my vision becoming hazy. My shoulders

were growing heavy, and it was getting difficult to stay upright. "When can I see Della?"

"Oh, you'll see her soon."

The sensation of soft makeup bristles against my cheek. A cool hand at my neck. My limbs went limp as Della's world disappeared and everything went dark.

Chapter Six

When I was growing up, we had a black-and-white border collie named Molly. She was sweet as can be, full of energy, and super smart too; too smart for her own good, my dad used to say. When we had to leave the house or if we had company over, sometimes my parents would lock Molly up in a dog crate. My older siblings used to think it was funny to lock me in the dog crate from time to time when we were playing around. They weren't being mean; it was just kid stuff. Only I didn't think it was so funny.

Memories of Molly the dog came to the front of my mind as I regained consciousness sometime later that day. Molly hated to be in her crate to the point where she wore down and broke off a few teeth. Eventually, Mom couldn't stand the way that she would hurt herself just trying to get free, so she got rid of the crate. We would put her in a bedroom or in the garage, but Molly still couldn't be contained. She could chew clean through bedroom doors and drywall, especially during thunderstorms or firework-centered holidays. Molly was a good dog. She deserved to live on a big farm herding sheep or something all day. She deserved better than to be stuck with our family.

My mouth was dry and cottony when I finally woke — I didn't know how many hours later. The parched, fuzzy sensation reminded me of the time in high school when I stole an edible from my older sister. That one little piece of chocolate had knocked me on my ass and made me so thirsty. This feeling felt similar to that experience, only ten times more intense, and as I slowly came back to reality, I only felt worse.

My lips were sealed shut with a thick strip of sticky tape wrapped around my head, making it difficult for me to breathe out of my nose. I struggled to move and realized my hands and feet were bound with the same silver tape that served to silence me. As I slowly gained consciousness, it became apparent that being gagged and bound wasn't my only problem. I was surrounded by a wire-grate cage — a dog crate, big enough for a large-breed dog or a hapless, pathetic nineteen-year-old. Panic seized my lungs as I attempted to scream.

"Oh good, you're awake."

I blinked through tears and glanced toward the vanity where it felt like I had been sitting only moments before. I stared at the back of a woman all dressed in black, her hair secured in some kind of mesh cap. She turned to face me, and shockwaves of disbelief constricted my chest as she opened her mouth to speak again.

"I have a live stream in fifteen minutes. I'm going to need you to promise not to make too much noise, or I'll have to drug you again."

Fresh tears cropped up at the corners of my eyes as I watched the woman place clear plastic tape strips at each cheekbone and under her jawline. The tape was connected to a series of clear strings that pulled her skin taut and hid along the mesh cap. With a swipe of purple lipstick and a dab of pink glitter at the apples of her cheeks, a familiar face slowly took shape before my very eyes. She placed a long, rainbow-colored wig on top of her head and turned to me with a smile.

"What do you think? Too colorful for a wellness-update video?"

I blinked, unable to think or move or do much of anything at all. Even if I could reply, I wouldn't have known what to say. This woman wasn't Della's mother after all. She was *Della*.

"I know, I know. The whole thing is a little bit Rainbow Brite. Do kids today even know who Rainbow Brite is? Probably not."

"Mmmm!" I moaned and kicked at the dog cage with my bound feet. I didn't know what the fuck was going on, but I did know one thing: I wasn't going down again without a fight.

"Shhhh!" Della said, raising a finger to her fuschia lips. "You already made me miss my first live stream. I need to post something today or else the algorithm is going to get all wonky."

"Mmmm-mmm!" I kicked at the crate again.

Della held up a small syringe and cocked her eyebrow. "Casey, please don't make me use this."

I breathed fast and hard through my nose and stared daggers at her across the studio. Anger and fear shuddered through my body as I sized up my situation. By all accounts, it seemed like my friend — my idol — wasn't who she seemed, and, even worse, had drugged and detained me for reasons that were unclear. I stopped wiggling and moaning as she held my gaze.

"Now, can I trust you to stay quiet? What is it that they do in the movies? Oh yeah — blink once for yes, twice for no."

I clenched my jaw and blinked once.

"Good. Okay, I'm going to make this quick, only about sixty seconds. You should relax and watch."

Della clicked on the ring light and positioned her phone. From my angle, I could tell that she was in the StreamVid app. Her face looked completely different in the camera than it had when I first met her that morning. Between the face tape and the filters,

CHAPTER SIX

Della's online persona looked closer to my age than she really was.

"Hey there, Della Nation." She pitched her voice higher and added a nasally vocal fry to her speech as she addressed the camera. "I just wanted to pop in and thank you so, so much for all of your kind words and support! As you can see I'm doing *so* much better!"

I lay there helpless as I watched Della complete her video, a storm cloud of questions rolling through my mind. What had I done to make her want to tie me up? Who was she really? And where the hell were my phone and keys? I remained quiet and still as Della gave her viewers a bogus health update that included a cocktail of expensive medicines, multiple doctor visits every week, and a promising prognosis. After what felt like an eternity of her cooing and blowing kisses to her viewers as they showered her with likes and monetary gifts, Della signed off her live stream and closed out of the StreamVid app.

"Ugh. I only had a thousand viewers. I can't take a long break between posts again." Della slid her rainbow wig off, placed it on a head-shaped stand, and turned to face me. "So is this what you wanted to see?"

I blinked twice.

Della shook her head. "I knew it was a mistake to send you my real address. I appreciate the flowers and the coffee, but we have a real mess on our hands now, don't we?"

I blinked once.

"Tell ya what." Della opened her vanity drawer and produced a pair of small silver shears. "I'll take that tape off your mouth if you promise not to scream. My neighbors Gary and Judy are nosy as hell and come running at every little thing. I have no issue cutting out your tongue if I have to, so you're going to be good, right?"

I blinked once.

"Good. Okay, here we go."

Della opened the door to the dog crate, reached in, and began to cut the tape around my mouth. For a split second I imagined her plunging the sharp end of the scissors into my open eye, snipping my nostril, or actually cutting out my tongue. Instead, she ripped away the tape, taking a good portion of the delicate skin on my lips and some of my hair with it.

"Fuck." I coughed and sucked in ragged breaths of air. "That hurt."

"Look, I don't like this any more than you do." Della closed the cage door and returned to her vanity seat. "You didn't give me much choice."

"You didn't have to lock me up!" I groaned, my head still spinning. "Did you fucking drug me?"

"Yes — I have to protect myself too, you know. *You're* the one who came uninvited." She frowned, deep lines wrinkling her brow. "You should never have come here."

"No shit." A bitter, explosive laugh escaped from my lungs.

"What's so funny?"

"You're just a big fake!" I cackled, completely losing it. "I'm so stupid."

"Sweetie, everyone is fake online." Della took off the wig cap and face tape and pulled out a makeup wipe. "Anyone who says they aren't is lying."

"Yeah, but you're profiting off of it," I said. "And I was dumb enough to help you."

"Hey, I never asked for you to set up a fundraiser for me!" Della snapped, waving the pink-and-purple-stained makeup wipe in my direction. "*You* created this problem for us. Not me."

CHAPTER SIX

"Why are you doing this?"

"Doing what? Keeping you as my hostage?"

"No! Why are you tricking everyone into thinking you're someone you're not?" I said, deflated. If Della wasn't real, then what was?

"Casey, do you know how expensive groceries are these days?" she asked, removing a set of false eyelashes. "*So* expensive. Then there's private-school tuition, football gear for Mason, hip-hop dance lessons for Madison, our trip to the Grand Canyon, the payment on my minivan... it all adds up."

"You're not even really sick, are you?"

"Do I look sick?"

"Not on the outside." I frowned, still trying to come to terms with my situation. "You must be making hundreds of dollars a month. All from lying."

"*Thousands* a month," Della corrected me. "Well, most months. I made ten thousand last month alone. I'm on track to double that this month."

"So isn't that enough? Why keep tricking people into thinking you're sick?"

"Because sympathy pays, honey. I'm getting out of this hellhole as soon as my youngest kid is in college. I've got big plans, and I know this gig isn't going to last. I have to sock away as much cash as I can while the going is good."

My head throbbed as the woman I'd thought to be Della continued to undo her transformative makeup. As my thoughts began to sharpen and my mind cleared, I became highly aware of the fact that Della being a big faker wasn't the worst of my problems. Whoever she was, this person had gone to a lot of trouble to knock me out and tie me up. In the past, I would have felt helpless, sick, frozen. I couldn't be the meek little Casey that everyone thought me to be if I was going to get myself out of this situation. I had to think of a way to get through to her, and I needed to think of it fast.

"Please let me go," I said. "I won't tell anyone, I swear."

"That's an option." She shrugged. "Or I could just kill you."

A cold chill settled into my bones as I watched her casually file her nails. She was a liar, and a kidnapper I supposed, but was she really capable of murder? The sweet, encouraging social media star who up until just a few hours ago had been my role model and friend? I didn't want to find out. The realization that no one really knew exactly where I was hit me hard in that moment. My hands and feet were beginning to tingle from struggling against my binds.

I cleared my throat and mustered up a false sense of courage. "I told people where I was going. Killing me is a bad idea. You wouldn't get away with it."

"You're probably right about that." She sighed and put down her nail file. "Besides, getting rid of a body is a lot of work."

"So what now?"

Della rested her chin in her hand and looked up at the ceiling in thought. "What now indeed. Well, I can't keep you in Hercules's crate forever, now can I?"

"No."

"I can't exactly just let you go either," she said. "One person blabs to the internet about my real identity, and it's over for Della. So the real question is, what do you *want*?"

"I want to get out of this crate."

"Well, *obviously*. But we need to come to a compromise first."

"What kind of compromise?"

"How about this: I'll agree to give you half of whatever you raise in the FundFairy account in exchange for your silence."

CHAPTER SIX

Della picked up the shears again. "I'll have dirt on you, and you'll have dirt on me. We both get paid, and everyone is happy."

I blinked as a whole new terror flooded through my veins. Fifty thousand dollars was a ton of money. For a fleeting moment, I considered the possibility of a windfall like that and what it could mean for my future. That kind of money wouldn't pay for all of veterinary school, but it would help. I quickly came to my senses and shook off the notion. What Della was suggesting was fraud, through and through. I didn't want to die, but I didn't want to go to jail either. I needed to tell Della something to keep her happy though. I just wanted to go home.

"I have a better idea," I said, my gaze flicking to her ring light. "Teach me how to do it."

"Excuse me?"

"Teach me how to do what you do," I said. "Show me how to create a following and get my own fans."

Della let out a low, dark chuckle. "Don't you think if it was that easy then everyone would be doing it?"

"No deal, then," I said, bluffing. "You're just going to have to kill me."

"*Fine.* Fine, ugh." Della walked over to the crate again with the shears in her hand. She opened up the door and began to snip the binds on my wrists. "We don't have much time, though. I have to pick up the kids from school soon."

Chapter Seven

I don't know if I had ever truly been in physical shock before I met Della, but in those first few moments out of the cage I cycled through all of the feelings and emotions. Fear. Disbelief. Devastation. I had foolishly put so much faith and trust into this online persona — a stranger whom I knew nothing about. I had devoted so much of my love and time and energy to Della, and for what? It was all a lie. Nothing had been real — not Della, not our friendship. As I sat at her vanity and listened to her speak, a whole new emotion dug its hooks into me: anger.

"I know how this looks, Casey," she said. "I'm not a bad person, really."

"Oh yeah? Do good people lock up their friends in dog crates?"

"We were never friends," she scoffed. "I have at least fifty top fans. You just happen to be one of them."

Della returned the scissors to the drawer. I clenched my jaw and hugged my knees as a ball of shame rose in my throat. I swallowed it down and wiped at a fresh crop of tears. "Who are you?"

"My real name is Jennifer." She leaned against the vanity and sighed. "I'm nobody. Just a middle-aged mom who got lucky."

"How? How are you doing all of this? Aren't your kids on social media?"

CHAPTER SEVEN

She shook her head. "They don't pay attention to me. They do their own thing. Besides, I've blocked their accounts."

"What about your husband?"

"He's dead."

The fine hairs on the back of my neck stood up, and my eyes grew wide. *Dead.* Maybe she was capable of really hurting me after all.

Della smirked as my mouth hung open. "Oh, don't be so dramatic. I didn't kill him. He was a Tampa cop. Died on the job three years ago."

"I'm sorry to hear that."

"Don't be. We probably would have ended up getting divorced anyway. Honestly, it was the best thing that could have happened to me." She stood, opened the vanity again, and took out a small black book. "They found him in his car with his eyes gouged out. This was in his lap."

"What is it?"

"It's the key to my success," she said. "A guidebook of sorts."

"Like a social media handbook?"

"No. More like a grimoire."

She opened the book and turned it so the pages faced me. As I struggled to focus on the book, the texture of the air changed, as though something heavy was pushing down on the atmosphere. The strange characters on the page shifted and moved as a low, grumbling voice growled from inside the book.

I gasped and recoiled. "What the fuck is that?"

She chuckled and closed the book with a loud slap. "That's enough for now."

"Oh hell no." I pushed myself upright into a standing position. "I may be gullible, but I don't believe in *magic.*"

"Sit *down.*"

All the air left my lungs as an invisible pair of hands pushed me back down. I stared up at Della, speechless, as she wiped a bead of sweat from her brow.

"Please don't make me do that again. It takes up so much energy."

I closed my eyes and sucked in a ragged breath. "So, what, are you a witch or something?"

"I don't like labels. But sure, if you want to call me that," she said, her tone and expression indifferent. "The fact is that without the incantations in this book, I wouldn't be successful at all."

My gaze shifted back to the vanity drawer. My instincts had been telling me to run from Della's house from the moment I arrived. Now more than ever, I knew that I needed to get far, far away. Still, I had made a deal with Jennifer/Della. And part of me *was* curious.

"So you're saying if I read what's in the book, I can get what I want, too?"

She shrugged. "Maybe. It took me a long time to figure out all of the working pieces. The book requires certain... sacrifices."

"Like blood?"

Della's expression went flat and cold as she shook her head. "I wish it only needed blood."

"Del — Jennifer, I don't think I can do this," I said, panic rising in my throat again. "Please, just let me go home. I promise I won't say anything to anyone."

"It's too late," she said in a singsong voice. "You wanted to get to know Della? Well, now you know."

"Please don't do this," I begged.

"It's already done." She flicked her wrist and glanced down at her smartwatch. "Ah, shit, it's after two. I need to go get Mason and Maddy from school. You have to get back in the crate."

"No. No way. I'm not going back in there."

"Well, I can't trust you to stay here on your own."

"So take me with you," I said. "I'll ride along to pick up the kids."

"Not a chance. They don't need to know anything about my online life," she said. "I'll only be gone for twenty minutes. Just stay here. I'll lock the shed and come back with something for you to eat and drink."

I frowned and thought for a moment. I didn't like the idea of being locked up again, but I didn't want to go back in the crate either. At that moment, it didn't seem like I had much choice.

"Okay. I'll wait here," I said. "I need to text my mother and let her know I won't be home for a few more days. I'll need to call out sick at work, too."

"I'll do it." She pulled my phone from the side pocket of her yoga pants. "What's your password?"

I rolled my eyes. "One, zero, two, nine."

"Ten twenty-nine? My birthday is your phone password?" She snorted and began to punch in the code. "You really *are* obsessed."

"Not anymore." My face flamed. "Her number should be right there in my texts."

"Who's Sean?" Della turned my phone screen to face me. There were a couple texts from Sean asking if Spike could eat houseflies. Under any other circumstance, I might have thought it was cute. "You don't have some boyfriend who's going to come looking for you, do you?"

"No, he's my pet sitter," I said. "What are you going to tell my mom?"

"There it is," she said, scrolling through my messages. "*I'm going to be staying with my friend for a few more days. I just wanted to let you know.* SEND."

"Can I just have my phone, please? I need to call my work, too."

"All in good time." Della returned my phone to her yoga pants pocket and clasped the odd little black book to her chest. "I'm locking you in here now. I suggest you keep quiet while I'm gone or things are going to get ugly."

"I will," I said, swallowing hard. My mouth was a desert. "I'll stay quiet."

"Good." She nodded toward her vanity. "Why don't you try out some makeup looks while I'm gone? I'll give you some pointers and bring back something for you to wear when I get back."

"Okay."

Della looked over her shoulder one last time and paused. "What was it about Della you liked so much anyway?"

"I don't know," I moaned. "I think I was just lonely, and you happened to be there."

She pursed her lips and nodded. "Sounds about right. I'll be back soon."

With that Della opened the door to the shed and closed it behind her. The sound of a lock sliding into place confirmed that I was trapped once more. I pressed my ear to the door and listened for her minivan engine to purr to life before collapsing to the floor in tears. I was trapped in a shed somewhere in Florida by a madwoman who could change her mind and kill me at any moment. Even if I could escape, she had my phone and my keys. I would have to play her game a little while longer if I wanted to survive this ordeal and get back home alive.

After a good long cry, I sat down at the vanity and gave myself a once-over in the mirror. My features were plain, I knew that much was true, but I was no less attractive than Della or Jennifer or whoever she really was. I picked up a brand-new black lipstick and applied it, the skin on my lips still tender from being ripped by the tape. If she could enchant a following of millions, certainly I could too. Maybe I *could* learn from her. The question was whether or not I really wanted to. That was when I remembered.

The scissors.

Hope swelled in my chest as I opened the vanity drawer and found the silver shears in all their gleaming glory. I didn't want to have to use them, but I would if things got out of hand. I slipped the scissors into the side of my high-tops and went to close the vanity drawer when something familiar caught my eye. It was a small glass vial, not unlike the ones I remembered from when I was a kid and had to get my blood drawn at the pediatrician. I was just about to pick it up when I heard the sound of a key sliding into the lock once more. I closed the drawer and turned just as the shed door opened.

Della walked in with a box of cheese crackers and a can of soda in one hand and a large paper bag in the other. My stomach growled as she handed me the food and drink.

"These don't have drugs in them, do they?" I asked, popping the top on the can.

"No. Not this time." Her eyes narrowed as she appraised me. "Black lipstick, huh? I was right about using the goth angle on you."

"The goth angle?" I said, gulping down the sugary carbonated soda. "For what?"

"For your new online persona, of course." She smiled and handed me the paper bag. "Here, I brought you these."

I put the can of soda down and gave the bag a skeptical look. The way this day was going, there could have been bones or a dead animal or who knew what inside. I gingerly opened the bag and pulled out leather, mesh, buckles, and what could only be described as a studded harness. I held it up and gazed back at her with a quizzical grin. "What's all this?"

"Your wardrobe, of course. You're going to be Sorcha." She smiled. "My protégé."

Chapter Eight

For the next hour, Della worked to transform me from regular, everyday nobody Casey into Sorcha, ethereal gothic princess. In another timeline, getting a makeover from Della would have been a dream, the prospect of appearing in a live stream with her impossible and out of reach. But now that it was actually happening, all I wanted was to escape. I was in a nightmare that I had created all on my own. A nightmare that I'd almost welcomed.

Della's plan was to set up a new account for me under the name SorchaSays and to use that new account to begin gaining followers. She would show me what hashtags to use, what filters and backgrounds and sounds were most popular, and how to work the algorithm to my advantage. With her endorsement, and a few cohosted live events, I would soon be up and running with my own revenue-earning StreamVid channel. Only I didn't plan on continuing the charade once I got home. *If* I ever got home.

By this point, I had been detained in the shed for hours, and it didn't take long after finishing my soda for my bladder to complain. It was likely near dinnertime, and it occurred to me that it had probably been twelve hours since I had last used the restroom. Even though the shed was hooked up to electricity, I didn't think it also had indoor plumbing. I legitimately needed to go, but I toyed with the notion that an urgent bathroom break could be my opportunity to escape.

"I need to pee."

Jennifer, now dressed in her full Della persona, hovered behind me as I struggled to fit into the black corset. She pulled the strings tighter and let out an exasperated gasp. "Well, you should have mentioned that before I strapped you into this thing."

"Sorry. I'm really nervous."

I sucked in a breath as my breasts heaved atop my crushed rib cage. Della finished tying me up as I gazed at my reflection in the mirror. For the last hour she had been working her magic, contouring my features with heavy makeup, applying false eyelashes and tucking my bleached strands of hair away under a jet-black bobbed wig. When she was finished, I barely recognized myself.

"Hold on," she grumbled, and moved to the far side of the shed to pull back a curtain just like in *The Wizard of Oz*. "You're in luck. When I moved all of the junk out of here into the house to set up my studio, I kept a few things around just in case."

After a moment of cursing and throwing items around, Della turned to face me with a bright orange five-gallon bucket. "This should do."

"You want me to pee in a bucket?"

"Well, I can't very well let you in the house. Not with the kids home anyway," she said, reaching for a box of tissues. "Here."

I winced and placed the bucket on the ground. Another humiliation. Della propped her hands on her hips and watched, impatient. "Well? Hurry up."

"Can't you turn around?"

CHAPTER EIGHT

"No."

I sighed and shimmied my tights down to my knees under the tulle skirt that she'd made me wear. I hovered over the top of the bucket, so eager to relieve myself that I didn't even care anymore if she watched.

"You know, there are certain streaming sites that would pay big-time to watch this," she snickered.

"Gross." I grabbed a tissue to wipe, tossed it in the bucket, and pulled up my tights again. "Thanks, I guess."

"You'll thank me later when you're making thousands of dollars a month on StreamVid," she said, clapping her hands together. "Okay, let's do this thing."

Della cleared her throat and powered on the ring light. We were a strange-looking duo, Della all bright and cheerful, in her lavender wig and iridescent gown, next to me looking like a goth princess. She had rolled down the green screen on the wall behind us and set the background to a dreamy watercolor galaxy motif. She scheduled the live stream countdown and gave me a stern look.

"Don't fuck this up."

I held my breath as the timer counted down. *Five, four, three, two, one.*

"Hey there Della Nation! I am so pleased to introduce you to my new friend tonight! Everyone, meet Sorcha! She's a real sweetheart and so full of light and positivity. I just love her!"

I blinked, my expression frozen. I had seen so many of Della's live streams before, and had made enough StreamVids of my own. Yet hooks of fear gripped into my chest as I struggled to think of something clever or witty to say. Nothing came.

"Aw! She's so nervous! Della Nation, give my friend here some support! Show her she's welcome!"

A flood of emojis and comments lit up the screen. Coins, flowers, and other monetary gifts poured in as Della simply stood there, blowing kisses and giggling.

"Oh, thank you so much, Jasper82! We love you, too!"

I struggled to keep up with the comments as one after the other populated the screen. I wasn't cut out to be a streamer, not on this level. I held up my hand and waved. "Hi, CherryMerryMuffin. Hi, BobsledIndigo. Nice to meet you all."

"That's the spirit!" Della giggled and held her hands to cover her mouth. "Now, I want you all to follow Sorcha. She's been working so hard behind the scenes to help me feel better. That's all for tonight, but if you want us to live stream together again soon, be sure to drop in a comment. And if you're new here, be sure to follow, like, and subscribe!"

Della blew another series of kisses into the camera and ended the live stream as I waved like a rigid robot. When she was certain that the streaming session had ended, she pulled off her wig and faced me, lips curled back and eyes flashing.

"What the fuck was that?"

"I'm sorry, Della," I said, my voice tight. "I don't know how to do this."

"Whatever," she sighed, readjusting her face tape. "Here, let's see if you got any new followers."

I peered over her shoulder as she clicked over from the Della Official account to the new Sorcha account. That afternoon when we'd first set it up, we had zero followers. Now, after a five-minute streaming session with Della, the SorchaSays account had already gained almost a thousand followers and climbing.

"Not bad," she said, pushing past me. "Now to make it stick."

"Make what stick?" I said. "That was a good start, right? I don't have nearly that many followers on my normal StreamVid account."

She pulled a stick of sidewalk chalk from her pocket and licked her lips. "Just stand over there for a minute."

I watched, confused, as she began to trace a five-pointed star onto the floor of the shed. A knot formed in my stomach as she stood and grabbed a box of candles from her table of props.

She glanced at me and pointed to the floor. "Lie down."

"No. Nope. Uh-uh," I said, backing toward the door. "This is sketchy."

"Oh, calm down. It's just going to be for one of your StreamVid posts," she said. "Witchy shit is really popular right now. You have to make witchcraft your angle."

"Oh," I said, still not completely sold. I didn't believe in supernatural stuff, but still, the sensation of invisible hands on my shoulders had definitely been real. It wasn't like I had many other options. I just wanted to finish this thing with Della and go home. Against my better judgment, I lay down in the center of the pentagram. My thoughts rushed back to the handful of sleepovers I had gone to in middle school where we'd attempted to summon demons and make each other float in the air. None of it had worked back then. I didn't expect it to work now.

Della placed a battery-operated candle at each point of the star, repositioned her wig on top of her head, and pulled the little black book from before out of the vanity drawer. Something hissed and hummed through the shed, like the sound of an air conditioner kicking on, as she opened the book. She fired up the ring light again, positioned her phone so that it was pointed toward me, and began to recite something from the book.

"*Azgoth*," she began. "*Maldrax.*"

The hum grew louder and a tingling sensation rippled through my body. A soft green light seeped through the floorboards of the shed, casting the room in an unnatural glow. It felt as though the air had been sucked out of the room as she continued her chant. My ultra-tight corset was already making it difficult to breathe, but now I was positively smothered.

"Della!" I gasped. "What the fuck is going on?"

"*Gorgoroth!*" she shouted, and pulled a knife from her dress pocket. "*Moldoor!*"

Up. I've got to get up. I tried to move, but something kept me pinned to the floor. My gaze shifted from the gleaming knife in her hand to the ceiling. Where there was once a set of wooden beams overhead was now a black, swirling void.

"Let me go, Della!" I pleaded. "You don't have to do this!"

"*Rakeesh!*"

With the last incantation, Della's eyes grew wide and wild. Her dark pupils had expanded as the whites of her eyes disappeared into their sockets. Her lips drew back into a fiendish grin too wide for any normal person, displaying rows of sharp needle-like teeth. I needed to do something, anything, but I was petrified and frozen in place like the prey animal I was. It took every ounce of strength I had to bend my knee as she held the knife high.

In one swift move, I pulled the pair of scissors I had hidden from my shoe and plunged the blades into Della's ankle. Her flesh opened up and a stream of blood shot out in a crimson arc as I twisted the handle. She let out a piercing yowl and recoiled as the demonic expression melted from her face. Whatever had its hold on me released in that moment, and I scrambled to stand upright.

"You're ruining everything!" Della screamed, the knife still clutched in her hand. She bent over and removed the scissors, letting out another scream of pain. I froze up again as she

CHAPTER EIGHT

hobbled toward me, dragging her bleeding foot.

My calf nudged against the makeshift bathroom bucket as I backed into the wall. Without thinking, I picked up the bucket and tossed the contents — urine and tissue paper and all — right at Della's face. She doubled over, crying and clawing at her face, her wig lopsided and wet. With my last bit of strength, I kicked her legs out from under her, and a whole new surge of adrenaline pumped into my veins.

She mewled and coughed on the floor, stunned and wretched as I contemplated my next move. My gaze rested on the dog crate where she'd held me captive only a few hours before, and I knew exactly what I had to do. I pulled her across the floor, her sparkly party dress wiping away the pentagram chalk lines as I stuffed her petite but powerful frame into the crate. I only took a moment to gasp and catch my breath as she moaned and writhed.

"Where's my phone and keys, you crazy bitch?"

"Why should I tell you?" Della laughed and coughed all at once.

"Because if you don't, I'll expose you. I'll tell everyone all about you!"

"On the table. Front hall."

I didn't wait around for Della to start monologuing. I kicked the shed door open and ran out into the night. A symphony of insects chirped as I whipped through the tall grass, past the pool lagoon, and over the cluttered porch. A blue light glowed from within the darkened interior as I slid the glass door open and stepped into Della's house again. I pushed my way past the tower of magazines and into the living room, where a television was on. There on the entryway table were the flowers and coffee that I had brought that morning, along with my phone and keys, just like Della said. I zeroed in on my belongings, determined not to stop until I was in my car and driving away from this nightmare.

I grabbed my phone and keys and had closed my hand around the doorknob when I heard a sneeze. My body went numb as I turned to see the little girl from that morning nestled amongst the stacks of laundry on the couch. She had a bowl of ice cream in her lap, and her Della-esque features were screwed up into a confused sort of expression. At that moment, I wanted to take her with me and rescue her from this hellhole of a nightmare house. But I needed to save myself first.

I held a finger to my lips and shook my head. "Whatever you do, don't go in the shed."

A piercing scream ripped from the little girl's lips as the ice cream bowl clattered to the floor. Hercules the dog barked from somewhere deep inside the house, and my dead limbs activated once more. I opened the door, stepped outside, and slammed it behind me just as the heavy body of a large-breed dog collided with the other side of the door. I sprinted toward my car, still parked across the street, and didn't look back.

Chapter Nine

I drove and drove and drove that night, holding back a flood of tears, until I crossed the Florida state line into Georgia. It was after midnight when I pulled into a well-lit truck-stop gas station just outside of Valdosta and finally allowed myself to collapse. I had driven for four hours straight, the last fifteen minutes on pure gas fumes, determined to get as many miles between myself and Della as possible. I was still processing all of the stages of shock and grief, but now I was more clearheaded than ever.

I rummaged through my overnight bag, found a wrinkled T-shirt to slip over my corset, and wiped off as much makeup as possible. I had ditched the black wig, but Della's professional makeup job was staying put. I did my best to wipe off most of it before entering the gas station, but I still looked awful. I needed to pee, eat, and refuel before I made the trip back home, and no amount of smeared eyeliner was going to stop me. The old me would have been too shy to go into a gas station looking like a hot mess in the middle of the night, but after my face-off with Della, some of my inhibitions had worn off. I had stared into the eyes of the devil; a few funny looks from locals weren't going to scare me now.

After relieving myself, I used the bathroom soap and paper

towels to wash off more of Della's makeup. The girl that stared back at me in the mirror now was more familiar, but different somehow; there was disappointment behind her eyes, and something else, too. Anger? Rage? Whatever it was caused my features to look just a little harder around the edges than before. I kind of liked it.

I picked up a bottle of water, two energy drinks, a bag of chips, and a package of cookies and brought them to the counter. The attendant behind the register was an older man who had likely seen worse than me in the middle of the night and didn't even bat an eye as I paid for my purchases. I refilled my gas tank and set my course for home.

I drove straight through the night, chewing on cookies and chips and wondering how everything had gone wrong. Should I tell my parents, or the police? Would anyone even believe me? I wouldn't even know how to explain what happened, or what to report. It sounded ridiculous even thinking about it. The color of the sky began to change as I coasted back into town, on fumes again, too tired to continue thinking about consequences or a course of action. I was back in my bed and fast asleep by the time the sun rose, but I didn't sleep for long.

"Casey! Hey, is everything okay?" My mom sat on the side of my bed and rubbed my back.

I sat up and threw my arms around her neck, exhausted and overwhelmed. All of the sadness I had been holding on to burst from my chest like a dam as I crumpled in her arms. "I'm so glad to be home."

"What happened?"

I hiccuped and wiped at my face. "My friend... she wasn't who I thought she was."

"Oh, baby. I'm so sorry," she said, squeezing my hand.

"I'm sorry I'm so shitty to you sometimes," I sobbed. "You're a good mom."

"Shh," she said, enveloping me in her arms again. "It's going to be okay."

Okay.

How could I ever be certain that things were going to be okay? My thoughts turned to my phone, to everything that had happened, to Jennifer/Della. Maybe I wasn't as safe at home as I thought. It was easy enough for me to find Della, but would Della try to come after me?

* * *

I slept all that first day back home, trying to put my experience with Della behind me. There were so many questions left unanswered, so many loose ends I needed to tie up. I decided that the best thing would be to lie low for a while, to be cautious and careful. Even though I hoped that she would stay away, Della was dangerous, and I didn't want to have anything to do with her. I closed down the FundFairy account and returned the donations to her fans; then I closed my StreamVid account and wiped out all of my other social media channels. I needed a clean slate. I knew that I would never be able to fully get Della out of my mind, but this was a good start.

One thing that I did want to keep from my bizarre experience with Della was the Sorcha hairstyle. My natural hair color was almost that dark anyway, and I was in need of a cut. I went to the drugstore the following morning, bought a box of dark brown hair dye, and gave myself a trim. When I was finished, I had to admit that the look suited me. Somehow, Della had instinctively known that deep down, this was who I was meant to be.

Sean texted me on the way in to work that day, asking if he should bring Spike. I missed my little guy, but was also surprised to find myself eager to see Sean, too. My ordeal with Della had made me realize that it was time to stop chasing imaginary friends online and to focus on the real people right in front of me instead. Only I was beginning to wonder what was real and what was fake, and if there was anyone I would ever really be able to trust again other than myself.

"*Casey?* Whoa, cool hair." Sean greeted me at work later that day with a cheesy grin. "Looks very French."

"Thanks." I patted my newly cropped hairdo. "Did you bring Spike?"

"Yeah, he's in the break room," he said. "How was your trip?"

"Don't ask." I rolled my eyes. "It was... bad."

"That sucks. You didn't have a good time with your friend?"

"No. Not at all." I chuckled. "I'm just happy to be home."

"I was gonna ask, did you delete your StreamVid account?"

"Yeah." I frowned and tilted my head. "Why?"

"Well, I was following you and I wanted to send you this bearded-dragon video, but I couldn't find your account."

"You were following me?"

He cocked his head and gave me a blank stare. "I'm YaBoiSean69? I've liked a bunch of your posts. I figured you knew it was me."

"Oh." Heat crept up my neck. "I didn't realize you were following me."

"I guess that's what I get for using an avatar." He shrugged. "Anyway, thanks for letting me hang with Spike. He's so cool. I can't wait to move into my own place so I can get a beardie of my own."

"You're getting your own place?"

CHAPTER NINE

"Yeah, I just signed the lease. It's closer to the college, anyway. I'm pretty stoked."

"Congratulations. That's so cool," I said, checking the time on my phone. "My shift starts soon."

"That's okay. I was gonna ask, do you still have time to go get that coffee? Like, maybe Friday?"

"Definitely." I smiled.

"Nice." Sean held up both of his hands, looking for a double high five.

I gladly obliged and laughed as we touched palms. "Oh my god. We're such dorks."

"Cool dorks." He pointed at me with double finger guns. "See you Friday."

"See ya."

My cheeks hurt from smiling as I entered Pet Planet that day to begin my shift. I was still reeling a bit from the ordeal at Della's, but I also felt a little freer in a way. Without StreamVid and all of my other social media obsessions holding me back, maybe I could start living life for real. College. A potential boyfriend. There were so many things I was missing out on by hiding from the world. Maybe I was finally ready to come out of my shell after all.

I set Spike up in the break room, clocked in, and took my place behind the counter, instantly reverting to the muscle memory of my phone. I glanced at my reflection in the glass screen, hardly recognizing myself. I was a new person. It was a new day. I powered off my phone, picked up one of my manager's tattered paperbacks, and read.

By the end of my shift at Pet Planet, I was almost feeling back to my old self. I was tired, as usual, but I was also keenly aware that the situation with Della had forced me to grow up somehow.

I walked a little taller; I felt a little more confident in myself. I'd driven all the way to Florida and back. I'd gotten myself into and out of a bad situation. If I could survive becoming a social media sacrifice, then veterinary school should be a piece of cake.

That night after my shift was over, I buckled Spike's travel crate into the back seat and turned my phone on again. It was definitely freeing to not feel the need to constantly have a device in my hand, to no longer equate my worth with a notification icon, likes, or a social media mention. For a split second I even considered going completely old school and getting rid of my smartphone all together — but I was probably going to need it for school. That was when I saw it: a message. From an unknown number.

My pulse picked up speed as my finger traced along the glass to open the message. The text was a short sentence, just four words, but it was enough to send a shiver down my spine.

We're not finished yet.

I blocked the number, deleted the message, and started my car. I'd been half expecting her to text or call me at some point. She'd had my phone in her possession long enough to find my phone number or email, so I wasn't surprised. Still, Della was clearly sending a threat, one that I had no intention of acknowledging.

As far as I was concerned, Della and I were finished. Only she was far from through with me.

Chapter Ten

Days turned into weeks as I slowly became more relaxed in the wake of my incident with Della. Sean and I began to meet regularly for coffee before my shift at work, and I grew completely smitten with him. He was funny and cute and easygoing, the kind of friend I needed. We didn't like the exact same things, but I enjoyed his company, and he was always there to return a text or a smile. After about a month of coffee dates, we shared a mint-gum-flavored kiss in the Pet Planet parking lot, and he officially became my boyfriend. It felt nice. It felt like more than I deserved.

College classes began on a crisp January morning, and with every passing day, my focus began to sharpen and shift. I discovered that I actually enjoyed the routine of getting up, getting ready, and having somewhere to go. It was a bit of a struggle to get used to doing classwork again, but the rusty cogs in my brain were eager to be used up on something other than scrolling through social media feeds and obsessing about people I didn't know. I was doing well. Until I saw Della, that is.

At least, I thought it was her. Rainbow-colored hair was still rare in my small rural town, but not completely unheard of. Still, when I saw the flash of purple-pink-and-green locks from across the courtyard at school, my heart skipped a beat. They say that trauma is held in the body, and at that moment, I knew it to be true. My knees turned to jelly and nearly collapsed under my weight as I watched the head of technicolor hair weave in and out of the crowd. At that moment, I was convinced that she had found me. Somehow, she'd figured out where I lived, and *she was coming for me.* The terror of what she would do rippled under my skin in waves, and for a brief moment, I felt the urge to puke, run, hide. But the terror quickly merged into something buried bone-deep when it came to Della. I shed the sense of fear and replaced it with rage.

I walked on shaky legs past the sea of smiling, laughing students toward the brightly colored head of hair. If Della wanted to have it out with me, then so be it. I wasn't going to run. I pumped my arms and breathed fast and heavy through my nose like a bull zeroing in on a matador. She wasn't going to get the best of me on my own turf. Not now. Not ever.

"What do you think you're doing?" I stood behind the rainbow-haired person, ready to strike. I was a viper. A once-caged animal with nothing left to lose.

"Huh?" The person turned to face me, and my heart dropped.

The expression on my face must have been terrifying. Rage bubbled just beneath the surface, frothing at the corners of my mouth and piercing through my eyes. Only it was a misdirected emotion. The rainbow-haired person wasn't Della at all.

"I'm so sorry!" I said, clasping my hand to my mouth. "I thought you were someone else."

"Weirdo." They scoffed and walked away.

I stood there in the courtyard, lost and unsure again. Maybe I hadn't shed Della completely from my system after all.

* * *

CHAPTER TEN

"How were classes?"

Sean sat across from me in our usual booth at the café and took my hand in his. His palms and fingers were warm from the coffee, and I was grateful for his touch. I was still shaken from the almost-encounter with Della. I was angry and terrified all at once. I couldn't hold in what had happened between me and Della any longer. I needed to get it out.

"School was fine, just... there's something I need to tell you."

"Hey, Carrie." I tore my gaze from Sean's concerned expression to see Marco smiling down at us. It had been a while since I'd thought about Marco. With everything that had happened, my little crush on him was nearly forgotten.

"It's Casey," I reminded him.

"Yeah, that's right," he said.

"So what's up?"

"I was just here to see some friends," Marco said, shooting me a flirty grin. "I put my notice in here a few weeks ago. Gonna start focusing more on my music."

"Oh. Cool," I said, flicking my gaze back to Sean.

"So, you're pretty famous these days, huh?"

"Excuse me?"

"Ah, come on." Marco smirked, taking out his phone. "SorchaSays? You're all over the place."

The earth seemed to open up beneath my feet as he turned his phone screen to face me. Marco had the StreamVid app pulled up to the SorchaSays account that Della had created. I blinked, shocked to see that the account still existed. When I'd left Della, the SorchaSays account only had a thousand followers; now it had nearly a million.

"That's not me." I shook my head and pushed his phone away. "Listen, Marco, I'm with someone here. Can you excuse us?"

"Uh, it totally *is* you," he said. "I didn't know you were friends with Della. She's a huge deal."

"I'm *not* friends with Della!" A huge burst of rage-induced energy flowed from my chest in a pulsing wave. Every cell in my body tingled as if my veins and nerves were made of lightning. In that moment it felt as though I could have melted Marco with my eyes.

Marco jumped and held up his hands. "Fine! Fine, it's not you."

"She said she wants to be left alone." Sean rose to his feet, his fists curled at his sides. I gasped as his usually jovial expression turned blank and cold. I had seen that expression before on Della. My heart sank as I realized that maybe I didn't know everything about Sean that I needed to know either.

Marco chuckled and shook his head as he turned to walk away. "Whatever, man."

I let out a long, slow sigh as Marco walked out the café door and Sean and I were left alone again. My pulse was surprisingly steady and even, but the tingling rage sensation still crawled beneath the surface of my skin. Something was off. It felt wrong but also... *good*.

"What was that all about?"

I took a sip of my tea, trying to choose my words carefully. "That was what I was trying to tell you about."

"So, did you, like, date Marco or something?"

"No, nothing like that." I shifted in my seat.

"I never liked him," Sean said, his eyes dark. "He was always stealing from the store when he worked at Pet Planet."

"Really?"

"Yeah." He took a sip of coffee. "So what did you want to tell me, then?"

CHAPTER TEN

I folded my hands on top of the table, wishing I could backtrack. I was still shaken from the encounter with Marco and the realization that my unwanted alter persona was still out there. How could I even explain what had happened? Where would I begin?

"Well, the thing is, I *am* SorchaSays. But I didn't really want to be."

"Okay." Sean frowned. "I still don't get it."

"When you watched Spike for me, I went to visit Della. She kind of... forced me into doing it."

"Oh." Sean's eyebrows raised. "I thought you weren't doing the social media thing anymore?"

"I'm not. After my visit with Della I decided to give it up." I leaned forward and lowered my voice to whisper, "Della's a psycho. I haven't told anyone, but while I was there, she locked me up and made me do this whole Sorcha thing. Then she tried to perform some kind of satanic ritual on me."

"Whoa, whoa, whoa." Sean chuckled. "She locked you up? Did you file a police report?"

"No." I shook my head. "It's complicated. Della is dangerous. She isn't who everyone thinks she is."

"All the more reason to go to the cops!"

"They can't help me," I said. "Anyway, I just wanted to tell you the truth. I'm trying to move on from it. I haven't told anyone but you."

"That's so weird," he said. "I'm sorry you went through that."

"Yeah." I snorted. "Me, too."

"Are you okay?"

"I think so," I said. "I was a little shaken up at first, and I thought I was over it, but now I don't know."

"What makes you say that?"

"I thought I saw Della at school today," I said. "It wasn't her. Still, it kind of feels like she's haunting me."

"So what are you going to do?"

I shrugged. "Nothing, I guess."

Sean took out his phone and held it up. "Mind if I do a little research?"

"No. But I don't need you to rescue me," I said. "This isn't your problem to fix."

"It's not my problem, but I care about you, and I want to help if I can." His eyes grew wide as he scrolled through the StreamVid app. "Boy, those posts are really popular."

"What posts?"

Sean passed his phone to me across the table. "The SorchaSays posts."

I glanced at the screen and began to scroll. There were dozens of posts tagging both me and Della asking for another collaboration. Della had posted the video of her incomplete ritual with the book and the pentagram. It was her most popular video yet.

PizzaSquish: OMG THAT'S CRAZY
B00bl3ss: is she ded
99Marbles: Della is unaliving her!
DellaFanClub: What is going on here?

Thousands of StreamVid followers had liked and shared the video, and as I scrolled through the comments, my anger grew again. I suppressed the urge to yell as I watched the video of Della's botched sacrifice. When it was over, I passed the phone back to Sean.

"Is there anything you can do to shut it down?"

"Maybe I can report the account to StreamVid." I shook my head. "I'd shut it down myself, but she set up the SorchaSays account. She's controlling it all."

"Are you worried that she's going to come after you or something?" Sean continued to scroll, raising his eyebrows suggestively. "This corset-dress thing you're wearing is kinda hot."

"Shut up." I gave him a playful nudge under the table. "No. I don't think she'll come here."

"Good. But if she does, just let me know."

I scratched my forearm as Sean continued to scroll on his phone. Maybe I was wrong to abandon the idea of being Sorcha. Whatever had happened at Della's might have all been just as fake as she was. For all I knew, I was turning down an opportunity to make a lot of easy money. The idea made me feel even more sick and unsure than before.

"I need to get home," I said.

"Yeah, I need to get back to work." He glanced up from his phone. "Are we still on for the movies tomorrow?"

"Definitely."

I walked Sean halfway back to Pet Planet and kissed him by my car. Itchy, burning waves crawled up my neck as he pulled away.

"Hey, are you okay?"

"Yeah," I said, scratching. "Just nerves. I'll be fine."

"Text me later?"

"Of course."

He waved and fell into a light jog toward the pet store as I slid behind the wheel of my car. My arms and neck itched like hell, and I was glad to be heading home. I glanced at my reflection in the visor mirror; angry red welts had populated all over my skin.

The house was empty and quiet when I got home, and I was

glad for the privacy. My mother would no doubt fuss over me if she saw the angry welts, and insist I go see an allergy specialist. I popped an antihistamine, found some hydrocortisone cream, and decided to lie down. When I opened the door to my bedroom, my heart skipped a beat.

Spike was not in his cage. Spike was on my pillow.

"What are you doing there?" I picked him up, careful to support his injured leg. He just stared back at me with his big, sweet eyes. I opened up his food box, picked up a fresh mealworm, and fed him before returning him to his perch. For a split second, the idea of placing one of the live wriggling grubs on my tongue crossed my mind. I shook the thought away, closed the lid to Spike's cage, and lay down on my bed.

I suppressed the urge to itch and scratch as I closed my eyes. I had homework and laundry to do, but the need to rest overtook me. The image of Della writhing and cackling in the dog crate dominated my thoughts as I finally drifted off into an allergy-medicine-induced sleep.

Chapter Eleven

I woke up early the following morning with a mouth full of cotton. I struggled to open my eyes, the corners crusted, my lids sealed shut. I rubbed my face and forced my eyes open as I sat up, disoriented and dizzy. I reached for my phone to check the time; it was just after six in the morning. I'd slept all afternoon and into the night. I had an early shift at Pet Planet anyway. Might as well get up.

I stumbled to the bathroom and slipped out of the clothes that I'd fallen asleep in, my arm tingling. I struggled to adjust to the light in the bathroom as I glanced down at my forearm. Red, scaly patches rose up in long strips where I had scratched. Maybe a trip to the dermatologist or at least the walk-in clinic would be in order after all.

My stomach rumbled as I showered, and it occurred to me that I had missed both lunch and dinner. I scratched at my neck as the warm water streamed down on me. The crawling, itching sensation built again. I considered taking another pink allergy pill, but I needed to open the pet store that day, and I knew it would just make me sleepy.

I got out of the shower and wrapped myself in a towel, itching and scratching as my stomach growled. The light over the bathroom vanity flickered and fluttered as I wiped the condensation from the mirror. The same raised, scaly patches ran up and down my neck. I dried off and dressed, layering my only turtleneck underneath my Pet Planet polo shirt. The combination of turtleneck and collared shirt looked ridiculous, but I couldn't go to work looking like a zombie either. I slipped out of the house just as the sun was beginning to rise, keeping quiet so I wouldn't wake my parents, my stomach complaining again. No time for breakfast.

I opened my car door and got in, and that was when I saw them on my dashboard: lying on their backs in a perfect row were six dead cockroaches. I sat there and stared at them for a moment, confused as to how they'd gotten there. Wondering *who* had put them there. I picked one up and examined its brown, shining body and spindly legs, and my mouth salivated. I held one to my lips and bit down, crunching on the exoskeleton. Its insides gushed into my mouth, and I gagged.

I opened my car door and spat out the remnants of the cockroach onto the driveway, heaving. I clawed at my tongue, desperate to get the acrid flavor out of my mouth. I took a swig from an old bottle of water in my car, swished, and spat before scooping up the rest of the cockroach corpses and throwing them into the grass.

I panted and gasped as I slid back behind the wheel of my car, no longer hungry. What the fuck was wrong with me? I didn't have time to ponder. If I didn't get going, I would be late for work.

I stuck my key in the ignition, checked my rearview mirror, and screamed.

Della stared back at me, her mouth set in a shark grin.

You can't run from this forever.

CHAPTER ELEVEN

I turned to face her. The back seat was empty. I glanced at the rearview mirror again. Nothing. I gripped the steering wheel, my heart pounding. I didn't need a dermatologist; I needed a psychologist. I threw the car into reverse and headed toward work.

* * *

I remained on edge all through my shift, trying my hardest not to scratch at my forearm and neck. Della's twisted features in my rearview mirror stayed with me as I rang up fish food, dog beds, and hamster toys. I had worked so hard to get Della out of my head, but I was losing my grip on reality again.

I was starving by the time Reagan came to relieve me for my lunch break. All day I found myself wanting to snack on the various insects and grubs that customers would purchase for their pets. This fact didn't disturb me nearly as much as the lesions on my skin. The areas that had already crusted over were peeling and healing to reveal smooth, scaly textured skin. I knew that I couldn't let this go on forever, but I didn't know what else to do.

I walked to the café, grabbed a premade sandwich, and sat on a bench in the sun. It was a chilly day out, but the sun was shining for a change, and I basked in it. I set my sandwich on the bench and resisted the urge to scratch, desperate for a distraction. I had to admit that I was curious about what people were saying about my StreamVid appearance as Sorcha. Before my meeting with Della, I would have done just about anything to have the kind of notoriety that she had. I caved, downloaded the app, created a new fake account, and began to scroll as I ate my sandwich in the sun.

I typed "Della" and "Sorcha" in the app's search bar, not entirely sure of what I was going to see. Immediately, dozens of videos came up of streamers just talking about the mystery behind what happened to Sorcha. Most of the videos were former fans of Della, each of them spouting off their own take on what was really going on. Many of the streamers questioned where I'd gone, and some of them even recognized me as Sorcha by my former AnimalLvr account. Some of the streamers thought it was all an act on our part, but others were worried about my whereabouts and also questioned what had happened regarding the FundFairy account. There were hours and hours of videos posted by Della's fan base demanding that she post an explanation as to where I had gone and looking for proof that she had ever even been sick.

I clicked over to Della's profile to see if she had answered any of their questions. She still had over a million subscribers, but the number of her followers seemed to be considerably less than I remembered. It appeared as though she hadn't posted any videos after our initial meeting except for one. The title of the video said "DELLA EXPLAINS IT ALL." My hand shook as I placed my sandwich on the bench next to me, swiped my finger across the screen, and clicked on the video.

"Hey there Della Nation," she said, dressed in her serious all-black Sick Della costume again. "I just wanted to address some of the things I've been seeing online. First, my health has taken a dive again, so I'm going to be offline for a while. I thank you all for understanding. Second, I wanted to let you know that as soon as I'm feeling better, Sorcha and I will resume filming together. I know that she's just as excited as I am to bring you some new videos like you've never seen before. Just hang tight while I'm in recovery, and I'll see you in my Streams!"

CHAPTER ELEVEN

Della blew a kiss to the camera, and the video started all over again.

I sighed. What was she up to? Perhaps she would find some other hapless fan and give them the Sorcha makeover? Maybe she was going to try to get me to do it again after all. Either way, I wasn't going to be a part of her fucked-up online games.

I turned to pick up my sandwich and noticed that a trail of ants had found my lunch. While I'd been plugged in to the screen, an army of little black ants had crawled onto my sandwich and begun feasting on the bread and cheese. I picked up the sandwich and admired the way they worked together, how systematically they kept in line, working together as a team to bring the goods back to the queen. Their hard little black bodies shone in the sun, and my mouth watered again. Without even thinking, I took another bite of my sandwich, wriggling ants and all.

I finished my sandwich, making sure to collect as many ants as I could. I scooped them up and tucked them into the bread, their crunchy bodies more palatable when hidden amongst lettuce and tomato. I licked at a few stray ants that had crawled up my sleeve before heading back to the store. I wasn't tired or hungry any longer, but I did feel something that I hadn't before; I felt powerful.

The rest of the day at work dragged on, my lust for eating insects temporarily quenched. My ribs began to itch, and I scratched through my double-layered shirts, trying to ignore the crawling sensation. Just before my shift ended, Sean ambled into the store, his cheeks pink and hair freshly cut. He was dressed nicer than usual, in a new T-shirt and jeans. He eyed me suspiciously as he headed toward the counter, and that was when I remembered why he was there. I'd almost forgotten that we had a date.

"Hey," he said, leaning against the counter. "You don't look so good. You still want to go out tonight?"

"Yeah. Definitely," I said, shaking my head.

"Really? Because we can go another time," he said. "You just look kind of tired."

"No!" I said, almost shouting. "I'll be fine, I'm just... having some kind of allergic reaction."

"Okay," he said. His expression told me that he wasn't so sure. "I'll wait for you outside."

"Okay."

Reagan relieved me five minutes later, and I retreated to the bathrooms to change. I had packed a nice dress to wear for our date, but my arms and neck were even worse than before. The sores were beginning to ooze and crust. I kept the turtleneck on and changed into the dress anyway, then reached for my makeup bag. I didn't wear a ton of makeup usually, but this was a special occasion. I zipped it open and gasped.

Inside was a brand-new tube of black lipstick. A tube of black lipstick that I *knew* I hadn't bought. It certainly wasn't a gift from my mother, either; she hated that I even dyed my hair, let alone wore nontraditional makeup. A sour, sick feeling bubbled in my guts. The cockroaches. The lipstick. Either someone was messing with me, or I was losing my mind.

I zipped the makeup bag closed and tossed it into my bag, my heart racing. *Fuck this and fuck Della.* I slung my bag over my shoulder and fast-walked out of Pet Planet and into the parking lot, where Sean was waiting for me, his black Mustang rumbling. I slipped into the passenger seat, rap music blaring from the speakers.

"Hey."

"Hey," I said, my eyes darting around the parking lot.

CHAPTER ELEVEN

"We can go another time if you're not feeling well, really…"

I leaned over and planted a kiss on his lips. "No. Let's go."

I wanted this one night with Sean to just be normal. I wanted to eat popcorn and watch a dumb movie, then make out with my boyfriend afterward and go home. I wanted—

Out of the corner of my eye, I saw a flash of white. Sean had barely had a chance to pull out of his parking spot when my entire body snapped to the side. A sound like an airplane and a train colliding filled my ears as the side of my head smashed into the window. Something popped in my face, and my seatbelt squeezed against my lap and chest. A low whine rang in my ears as I struggled to turn my head and look at Sean. His eyes were closed, and his airbag had deployed. The entire driver's side was crumpled in.

"Sean." I reached out for him, my voice raspy. "Sean, wake up!"

The passenger door opened, and I sensed someone undoing the buckle on my seatbelt. A pair of strong hands snaked under my arms, and I was pulled backward away from the wreckage as the world went black.

Chapter Twelve

My eyelids fluttered open sometime later that night as I was greeted by the familiar sound of tires on asphalt. My head bobbed as I struggled to lift it, my body in agony as though I had been in a car crash. My neck was stiff and ached; my vision doubled as I struggled to understand where I was. My hands were bound, and I was strapped into a bucket seat, fast-food wrappers and trash rustling at my feet. It smelled the way my mom's SUV had when I was a kid, which made sense; I was trapped in the back of a minivan.

"Ah, you're finally up." Della — or, rather, Jennifer — smiled at me in the rearview mirror. "Good thing, too. We're nearly to the state line."

"Wha the fa did you do to me?" I mumbled, my lips not working the way I needed them to.

"I might have given you a liiiittle too much painkiller. Sorry about that," she said. "I'll get you some caffeine at the next stop. That should perk you up."

"Take me back," I said, smacking my lips. "I need to go to a hospital."

"Oh, you'll be fine. Don't be such a baby."

My throat tightened and tears sprang to my eyes as the events of the afternoon came rushing back. The crunch of metal and glass. Sean's head tilted at an unnatural angle. Someone dragging me away. Della. Fucking *Della*.

"You killed Sean," I sobbed through fresh tears.

"He's not dead," she said, merging onto an off-ramp. "At least I don't think he is. Anyway, I did you a favor. Boyfriends are just a distraction, and you have a lot of work to do."

"I'm not doing any work with you," I said, my head clearing. Anger flowed fresh and fierce through my body in a sobering wave. "Take me home, Jennifer!"

"You might change your mind after I tell you what you need to hear." Della craned her head to read the signs on the off-ramp. "Cheeseburgers or chicken nuggets?"

"Neither."

"Hmmph. Doesn't surprise me."

I sat in my binds in the back seat of the minivan, seething as Della pulled into a fast-food drive-through.

"Listen, I don't want to gag you, but I will if I have to. Keep your mouth shut while I order."

I would do no such thing. The old Casey might have sat back and taken it, been too scared to make a move or advocate for herself. But not anymore. As soon as she pulled up to the drive-through menu, I waited for the speakers to crackle and made my move.

"Welcome to BurgerStop. What can I get you?"

"Help!" I shouted. "She's crazy! Call the police!"

A hand reached back and slapped at my mouth, and the prongs of one of Della's glittering princess-cut rings crashed into my teeth. I tasted blood and spat at the white-hot pain.

"I'll gut you on my next live stream if you say another word!" she whispered, then turned to the drive-through speaker, continuing in her normal singsong voice, "Sorry, that was my daughter. She's just messing around. Can I get a double cheeseburger, fries, and two sodas?"

"That'll be seven seventy-six. Pull through."

I pursed my throbbing lips as she pulled the minivan forward to the window. I was tempted to scream again as she paid for her meal, but the kid at the drive-through window didn't look the least bit interested. I didn't want to put the restaurant staff at risk either; I had already witnessed what she did to Sean. I didn't want anyone else getting hurt on my account.

Della pulled into an empty parking spot, got out, and opened the sliding side door, and I was finally able to get a good look at her. She appeared much as she had the first time I'd seen her, only a little more gaunt and unkempt. Her hair was longer, limp and greasy, and her eyes were wild, as though she hadn't slept or showered in days. She closed the sliding door, sat in the bucket seat opposite me, and opened the greasy paper bag.

"French fry?"

"No, thank you," I said, unsure why I bothered with pleasantries.

"So," she said. "I went to a lot of trouble to get to you."

"I can tell."

"I had to ask my parents to take the kids. What a nightmare," she sighed, shoving a fry into her mouth. "Being a single mom is rough, ya know?"

"No. I don't know," I said, avoiding eye contact.

"Well, I'm going to keep this brief, since you hit your head and all. You probably want to get some more rest."

"I didn't *hit my head*. You crashed into Sean's car!"

"Same difference," she said, taking a sip of soda. My vision narrowed in the low light of the darkened parking lot as I tried to get a better look at my captor. Della looked... older somehow.

CHAPTER TWELVE

The skin around her eyes and nose seemed to be flaking and dry. A dark caked spot at the corner of her mouth opened up and began to ooze as she bit into her meal. Something was wrong with her, that much was obvious — something more than just psychological.

"How are you even driving this van?" I asked. "Sean's car is probably totaled."

"I'm not *dumb*, Casey. I used your car," she said, her lips set into a smirk. "The cops are going to think that you and your boyfriend got into an argument, and you crashed into him. Easy."

I swallowed hard, every cell in my body numb with rage. Della sat next to me, munching on her fast food, relaxed and at ease despite the fact that she'd attempted to murder my boyfriend and kidnapped me. A small part of me still mourned for Della, for the kind social media friend who always knew what to say, who always gave me that sweet hit of serotonin I was looking for. An even bigger part of me seethed, determined to get justice for Sean, for myself, and for everyone else she'd hurt along the way.

"Anyway, here's the deal. You're going to come back with me and film a few more StreamVids to get my fans off my back. We'll let everyone know that Sorcha is okay, and then we can either shut down the SorchaSays account or you can keep with it. Your choice."

"My choice? If I really had a choice, I wouldn't be here right now."

"Casey, don't be a pill. You created this situation, and now you're going to help me get out of it," she said. "Besides, if you would have just answered my texts, I wouldn't have had to come and get you."

"Come and get me? You mean assault me and my boyfriend and then kidnap me?" I said, the words coming out in a half laugh.

"Would you have willingly come with me?"

"No."

"Well then, you see my problem." Della took another bite of her burger. "But then, I'm not the only one with a problem, now, am I?"

"What do you mean?"

"Feeling a little itchy?" she mused, examining a fry. "Find that you're having some strange cravings?"

My body went numb as I remembered the itchy patches on my neck and arm. The cockroaches. The ants. "You did that to me?"

"I told you, that little black book is powerful." She shook her head and took another sip of her drink. "I can fix it, but you need to help me first."

"And what if I don't?"

Della chuckled and shook the ice in her nearly empty drink. "Then you'll turn into the reptile that you really are."

* * *

Della wouldn't shut up for the rest of the drive. At times, I tuned her out, especially when she began to rant about algorithms and collaborations, sponsorships and followers. I'd never really given much thought to posting on StreamVid for anything other than fun; I hadn't ever wanted to chase followers, make a name for myself, or make money off of social media, and I sure as hell didn't now. Della, on the other hand, was obsessed.

"Did you know that you even have to post at specific times to maximize your views? It's crazy!" she said, exasperated. "But once you crack the algorithm, it's easy to have StreamVidders eating from the palm of your hand. You just have to give them what they want."

"And what is it that they want?"

"Attention."

* * *

It was still dark as Della pulled into her neighborhood. Even in the low light, I could tell that her lawn was more in need of maintenance than before. My neck and arm itched like hell, and the entire ride home, her words kept ringing in my ears. *You'll become the reptile that you are.* What the fuck did that even mean? Did she really have the power to make me turn into a cold-blooded creature? I didn't want to find out.

"I'm not going to bother bringing you through the house this time. Hercules did *not* like you anyway. Don't be offended though; I trained him not to like anyone." Della opened the sliding van door and went for the seatbelt. I was weak from being drugged, and every inch of my body throbbed from the car crash, but still, I wanted to run.

As if she was reading my mind, Della stopped and held up a closed fist. Her eyes flashed, and the open wound at the corner of her mouth seemed even angrier than before. "Don't even think of trying to run away. I don't want to sock you in the jaw again, but I will. It's a real bitch to cover up bruises. Ask me how I know."

"Fuck you."

"Yeah, fuck you, too." Della undid the seatbelt and helped me out of the van, my hands still bound in front.

The minute I put weight on my legs, I knew that running away wasn't an option. I could barely keep myself upright. Despite the fact that she looked like she was falling apart, Della was strong enough to help me walk around the side of the house to the backyard. The tall grass scratched at my ankles as she moved with a noticeable limp, a fact that, despite my current situation, made me smile. I had hurt her once before; I could do it again.

"You're not going to put me in a dog crate again, are you?" I asked as we passed the destroyed pool cage and forgotten vegetable garden.

"No. If you're good, I might even let you pee in the house this time," she said.

The door to the shed was already unlocked as we approached, and terror flooded my veins. The trauma of being detained and tortured there by Jennifer/Della only a few weeks before came rushing back, and my already weak legs collapsed under me.

"Oh, don't you make me drag you again!" she huffed, snaking her hands under my armpits. "It doesn't have to be this difficult, Casey!"

"You sound like my mother." I dug my heels into the dirt. I might have been weak, but I wasn't going to make this easy for her.

"Really, I thought you would understand," she grunted, hoisting my body up the steps and into the shed. For someone so dainty and petite, she sure was strong. "There. See? No cage. If you just fucking *cooperate*, we can get this done and move on!"

Chapter Thirteen

"I probably shouldn't have let you live in the first place."

I sat tied to a folding camp chair, an unwilling audience as Della settled into her spot at the vanity. She pulled her hair up into a bun on top of her head, bobby pins pinched between her dry lips. The brilliant vanity lighting revealed that she was missing hair. The back of her neck was covered in lesions that looked similar to the one on the corner of her mouth. I shuddered as I realized they were the same lesions that had appeared on my arm and neck. By all appearances, it seemed as though Della was even more fucked up than me.

"Aaaanywayyyys," she said, dragging out the syllables. "I've got you back now, and we can finish what we started."

"I'm not finishing anything with you," I said. "You can rot and go to hell for all I care."

"Cool, but you'll be rotting right along with me," she said. "Once you begin a ritual, you have to complete it."

I seethed in my binds, trying to figure out a way to escape, a way to get through to her. My feet had also been bound with tape, though Della hadn't taken my bathroom needs into consideration again. While she was slathering a thick layer of foundation onto her cheeks, I quietly relieved myself, allowing the tape around my ankles to become soaked in urine and loosen.

I was able to free my feet without her noticing.

Even if my hands were tied to the camp chair, I could still run away at least. I wasn't going to wait around to stare into the black abyss again. It was cold and dark and lonely in there, and I didn't trust that Della wouldn't send me into whatever portal she and the book conjured up. The last time I'd been in her shed of horrors I was nearly sacrificed to... I didn't know what. All I knew was that I didn't want to find out.

"The cops are probably going to show up any minute," I said, wriggling my wrists. "You can't just crash a car into someone and get away with it. Besides, my mom is probably freaking out right now looking for me."

"No one is looking for you, Casey. I promise," she said. "Not here, anyway."

"What do you mean?"

"Well, the cool thing about social media is that you can set up as many accounts as you want. You can pretend to be who you want, post whatever you want. It was easy to set up a new StreamVid account under someone else's real name."

"You didn't."

"Police will be busy looking for you far from here. I've set it all up to look like you're heading out west somewhere," she said, putting the finishing touches on her makeup. "Anyway, I'm not too worried. Once this is all done, we'll both be happy, and everything will be as it should again."

"How can you say that?" I said, twisting my wrists. "Sean is probably dead! And even if he isn't dead, you'll still have to answer for hurting him and kidnapping me."

"You underestimate the power of the book, Casey," she said, dabbing extra makeup on the corner of her mouth. "After we perform the ritual, I'll be able to shift and bend reality any way

I want."

"Why didn't you just do this in the first place, then?" I said, a crazed laugh escaping from my throat. "Why bother with StreamVid at all?"

"Because, dummy," she said. "I needed to find someone gullible who would buy into all of this. I needed to find *you*."

I continued to watch as Jennifer slowly transformed into Della, one false eyelash and contoured cheekbone at a time. She slipped out of her yoga-pants-and-T-shirt ensemble and pulled on a multi-tiered chiffon dress with a pastel rainbow print and topped the whole look off with a purple wig. When she was satisfied with her hair and makeup, she pulled the little black book and the dagger from the vanity drawer and turned to me.

"Casey, if this is going to work, then you'll have to trust me."

I wiggled my toes, grateful to have sensation in my feet again. Whatever drugs Della had given me after the car crash must have worn off. My anger combined with a wave of adrenaline as she walked toward me, and I was overcome with a burst of energy. I knew that this time, I wouldn't just let her continue to use me. I wasn't going to sit back and take it anymore. This time, Della was going to pay.

"We just need to film one StreamVid. That's all," she said, bringing the knife to my wrist. "Just one little ceremony, and everything will be just as it should."

I held Della's stony gaze as she sliced through the layers of tape binding me to the chair. Even through film of makeup and with the aid of her usual beauty tricks, the deteriorating Jennifer still came through. As soon as I was free from my binds, my hand curled into a fist, sailed through the air, and landed in an uppercut on her chin. Della's jaw cracked and the screech of a wounded animal escaped from her lips as the knife clattered to the floor.

I stood on wobbly knees and kicked Della away from me with as much force as I could, my foot connecting with the soft center of her belly. She sailed across the room like a deranged rainbow and landed in a heap at the foot of her vanity. I reached for the dagger and closed my fingers around the handle, triumphant. I moved on sheer instinct alone as I cut the binds from my other wrist. I was turning toward the shed door, ready to run like hell, when I heard a sound I'd never wanted to hear again.

Azgoth.

My limbs seized, and all of the air left the room. Something heavy pressed on my chest as I struggled to glance back over my shoulder at Della. Her purple wig had fallen to the floor, exposing her patchy, diseased-looking scalp. Wisps of blond hair fell around her shoulder as she held up the little black book and continued to recite.

Morgoth.

My head snapped back, and the same green light from before filled the room. My arms shot out at the sides, and tears flowed from my eyes. This was it. I had tried and failed. She was going to sacrifice me to some social media demon. In that brief moment as my toes lifted off the shed floor, I thought about my family, about Spike, about Sean. I thought about veterinary school and the friends I would never get to make and the places I would never get to visit. I had let something so meaningless hold so much meaning in my life, and now I was going to lose it all.

Selaroth.

My feet lifted higher off the shed floor, my chin pointed toward the ceiling. The swirling black vortex had returned, filling my heart with dread. My arms extended further out at my sides as though something were trying to tear me apart, limb from limb.

CHAPTER THIRTEEN

A low, dull roar filled my ears, and I knew that my end was near.

Damoth.

And then a bright white light shone in my eyes, and a familiar voice cut through Della's incantations and the steadily growing growl that was bouncing off the floor.

"Casey?"

Chapter Fourteen

The green light that had filled the shed disappeared, and whatever had its hold on me let go as my body crumpled to the floor. It only took me a moment to regain my strength, because I knew the person who had opened it had come to my rescue. Standing in the doorway of the shed was none other than my mother.

"Casey! Baby, are you okay?"

"Mom!" I rushed into her arms, overcome with relief. A sob ripped from my chest as she stroked the back of my head. I didn't know how she'd found me, and at that moment I didn't care. All I wanted was to go *home*.

"What's going on here?"

"No time to explain," I said, grabbing her hand. "We have to go..."

"*No!*"

I glanced over my shoulder and gasped. Della floated just above the shed floor, her purple wig in a heap at her feet. The flesh on her face was loose and waxy, as though it were melting away from her skull. My feet turned to lead as my mother encircled my shoulder with a protective arm.

"We have to finish what we started," Della said, her words coming out in a frothy spittle. "She's mine."

"I'm taking my daughter home," my mother raised her chin,

her eyes narrowed. "She doesn't belong to you, or to anyone else for that matter. She belongs to herself."

"I've worked too hard for this!" Della screamed, and pointed the book at me. "*Vagoth*!"

My feet began to rise up from the floor again, but unlike before, my mother held tight and kept me from floating away. A low, rumbling growl filled the air as the black swirling vortex opened up overhead. The pressure in the room changed, and my ears popped as I held tight to my mom.

"Jennifer, think about your own kids," my mother continued, her voice calm and even. "They need you, too."

"*Azgoth*!" she screamed. "Wait! No, I meant *Azgaroth*!"

The same green glow that had filled the room returned again, but this time, it spilled forth from Della's open mouth. She sucked in a gasping breath like a fish out of water as the book dropped to the floor. More light spilled from her eyes and fingertips in lime-green beams. She floated closer to the swirling vortex ceiling as a series of gurgled grunts and yowls flowed from her mouth. A black twisting tornado of smoke snaked down from the ceiling like a finger and touched her forehead as she began to claw at her eyes. My feet hit the floor, and my mother didn't wait around to see what would happen next.

"Run." Mom took my hand in hers and pulled me out into the night. A low growl boomed from the shed as we hurried past the rusted-out pool cage, through the overgrown weeds, and into the front yard, where her SUV was idling. Without saying a word, I slid into the passenger seat, and Mom peeled out of the yard. I held on to her hand and wept silently as she drove us out of the neighborhood and back onto the highway. Once we were at cruising speed, she squeezed my hand, picked up her phone from the holder, and began to talk into her text app.

"I found her, Ed. On my way home." She placed her phone back in its holder and glanced at me. "I normally don't like to text and drive, but I needed to let Dad know you're okay."

"How did you find me?"

"I used the find-my-phone app," she said. "After the accident, the police were no help, so I decided to take matters into my own hands. They wanted me to stay home and let them do their job. I couldn't just sit at home. I had to find you."

"Is Sean..." I said, choking on the words. "Is he...?"

"He's okay. He's in the hospital. He got a bad cut on his head and his ankle is crushed, but he's stable," she said, her voice tight. She gripped the wheel and sobbed. "God, Casey. I'm so sorry."

"This wasn't your fault," I said. "Mom, I can't believe you found me."

"I'm partly to blame. Jennifer's an old rival of mine from back in the day." Mom's hands flexed on the wheel. "I thought she was done messing with people's heads, but some people never know when to quit."

"Wait, you *knew* her?"

Mom nodded. There was something different about her eyes, something I hadn't noticed before. "We'll need to go to the police as soon as we get home."

I nodded. "Okay."

"What was going on in there anyway? Voodoo? Witchcraft?"

"I dunno," I said.

"Casey, how did you get into this mess anyway?"

I sighed and stared out the window. Mom must have driven all through the night to come and get me; the sky was growing lighter. A new day. "I stopped paying attention to the real people

CHAPTER FOURTEEN

in my life who mattered. I trusted the wrong person."

"Well, we have a long drive home," she said. "Start from the beginning."

And so I told her everything, from the moment I first laid eyes on Della to the moment my mother had burst through the shed door. That drive home was the most one-on-one time I'd had with my mother in as long as I could remember. I hadn't realized how much I had missed her; even though we lived in the same house, I had shut her and everyone else out. Then and there, I decided that I would never shut my friends and family out again.

By the time we reached the state line, I was even laughing a little, and the itchy, scaly wounds on my arm and neck had healed. When we were out of Florida, I finally rested my head against the passenger window and closed my eyes. I was safe again, in the presence of someone who actually loved me and cared about me. I let my mother's careful driving lull me into a restful sleep, and I didn't wake up until we got home.

Chapter Fifteen

Four Years Later

"Sean, have you seen my cap? I'm going to be late!"

I rummaged through the pile of clean laundry on the chair in our bedroom, my green tasseled cap nowhere to be found. We had exactly one hour to get down to the civic center for my graduation ceremony, and I was almost on time for a change. Our apartment was slightly messy, but with both of us working and going to school, it was to be expected. Spike gave me a quizzical stare from his perch on our dresser as I continued to search for my things.

"Oh, you mean this?" Sean hugged me from behind and buried his face in my neck, the graduation cap in his hand. "It was on the kitchen counter."

"Thanks, babe." I turned, gave him a quick peck on the lips, and grabbed the cap.

"Nervous?"

"A little," I lied.

"You're thinking about her again, aren't you?" Sean held my hands and sat on our bed. My gaze flitted to the shadow of a scar over his eyebrow from the car accident all those years ago. It had taken a long time, but we were both healed from the incident

CHAPTER FIFTEEN

with Della. Almost healed, anyway.

"Can't help it. She's kind of always there," I said. "Always in the corner of my mind."

"I was going to wait until after the graduation ceremony to show you," he said, taking out his phone. "You're not going to believe this."

Sean opened up the StreamVid app, and my breath stilled. It had been years since I'd touched social media, and the interface of my once-favorite app looked completely different. I didn't miss all of the anxiety and stress that being chronically online brought me, but I did feel a little bit out of the loop at times. All of my new friends at college had social media accounts, but they understood why I stayed away. As one of the victims of the notorious Jennifer Martin, aka Della, aka the Deepfake Mommy, everyone who knew about my past handled me with kid gloves. Everyone except for Sean, that is.

"I really don't want to look at that," I said. "Sean, you know I don't care about that stuff anymore."

"I know, I wouldn't show you if it wasn't important. Just... check out this account."

Sean turned his phone to face me. It took a moment to figure out who the talking head on the screen was, but then it hit me. She was a blond and angelic-looking teenager with a petite frame and delicate features. Features that looked alarmingly familiar.

"Is that..."

"Della's daughter," Sean said. "After her mom disappeared, she started up a true-crime channel."

I watched as the teen talked into a tiny microphone with photos of her family in the background. She was telling the story of her own mother, Jennifer, the psycho social media deep-fake.

The video already had over forty thousand likes and thousands of shares.

"Here we go again," I said. "Prepare for the influx of harassing texts and emails."

"You know, if you just take my last name when we get married, your fans will leave you alone." Sean tossed the phone on the bed and pulled me down beside him into a kiss.

I kissed him back despite my perfectly finished hair and makeup and gave him a playful shoulder punch. "No way, I'm not giving in to the patriarchy because of a bunch of internet weirdos. Let's just make up our own last name."

"Like what?"

"I dunno," he said. "Something cool like Dragonslayer or Deathmaster."

"I don't think people will want to take their pets to Dr. Deathmaster," I groaned. "Okay, seriously. We gotta go or we're going to be late."

"She looks just like her," Sean said, picking the phone back up. "Don't you think?"

"Yeah." I sighed, remembering the little girl nestled into the cluttered couch. "It must have been hard on her and her brother, you know. Discovering that their mom was insane."

"Do you really think she's dead?" Sean said, clicking his phone off. "I mean, I know we've talked about this a bunch of times before, but sometimes I still wonder."

"She has to be," I said. "I saw the thing come out of the ceiling and reach for her. The police didn't find any trace of her. Besides, I think she would have come back for me by now if she wasn't dead."

"Sorry to bring it up. I just wanted to give you a heads-up in case," Sean said. "Are you okay?"

CHAPTER FIFTEEN

"Yeah. You?"

"I'm good," he said. "I think we've both come a long way."

"We have."

"I'm gonna go start the car. Meet you down there?"

I nodded. "Yeah, I'm right behind you."

I smoothed out my green satin gown and walked to the bathroom to fix my hair and makeup. The girl who stared back at me wasn't quite as naive as she used to be, but for the most part, I was still the same. I reapplied my lip gloss, blew Spike a kiss goodbye, and headed out the door.

Sean drove us to the civic center, some fifteen minutes away, where my parents and siblings were already waiting. I'd been surprised that everyone wanted to make such a big deal out of getting my four-year degree. Even though I had been accepted into the veterinary program at Florida State University, I still had a long way to go to complete my goal. It was weird to be heading back to Florida, but I was going to be glad for the change of scenery, and Sean and Spike would be by my side.

I kissed Sean goodbye and joined my fellow classmates behind the stage as he wandered toward the rows of seats. I was a bundle of nerves as I waited for my name to be called, and an old familiar feeling sank into my gut. Hot, itchy patches popped up on my neck and forearm as I approached the stage, and I had to resist the urge to scratch. I stepped onto the stage, and a huge palmetto bug crossed in front of me, skittering slowly as though it had been poisoned. My pulse picked up and my breath grew shallow as I heard my name being called over the speakers.

I gazed out at the rows and rows of seats, searching for my mother and Sean. I just needed to see them, to know they were there, and I would be okay. I bit my lip as I scanned the crowd, finally sighting Sean. He was making a huge fuss, fist-pumping the air and using his hands as a megaphone to cheer for me. My mom and dad sat next to him, smiling and clapping politely. Mom gave me a thumbs-up as I walked toward the dean, who was handing out our diplomas. My siblings were all lined up in a row next to them, one of my sisters with her nose in her phone, one of my brothers balancing my baby nephew on his lap. They were all there for me. And at the end of the row, smiling and clapping, was a woman with purple hair and a rainbow chiffon dress.

I continued to walk toward the dean in slow motion as I met Della's milky gaze. Her skin was sallow and drooping, her teeth black behind thin gray lips. She clapped with bloody hands, the flesh on her forearms ragged and drooping. Even after all this time, she was still trying to get to me.

You're not real, I thought.

I had done this so many times before. At school, on dates with Sean, at work. I never knew when she would appear. After the incident, Della had never really left me. She always wanted the spotlight, but I wouldn't let her have it. Not today.

Go away.

I broke into a smile as I reached the dean. I grabbed my hard-earned diploma, shook his hand, and turned toward the crowd. Lights flashed as the photographer took my photo, and spots floated before my eyes. I walked in a haze off the stage and back behind the curtain, where I knew she would be waiting for me.

"Congrats, Casey!"

"Congrats!"

"Congratulations!"

"Thanks!" I said, hugging my fellow classmates, trying to tame the terror that was building in my chest. I hunched over and caught my breath, my face burning like fire. I knew what was coming, and I had to prepare myself.

"So, big graduation day. On your way to veterinary school, huh?"

I turned slowly, knowing that I really shouldn't interact with her. It was what she wanted. Even after all this time, she was still hungry for attention. Still, this was my day. My graduation ceremony. My rules. It was time to put Della to bed for good.

"You weren't invited."

"Such a shame." Della took a drag from a cigarette, a plume of smoke encircling her wretched features. "You could be making so much money on StreamVid right now. I bet you've got student loans out the ass."

With each passing year, Della grew more and more grotesque. After the incident, I hadn't told Sean or my mother or my therapist or anyone that I still saw her. I didn't want to worry them, and I knew how to make her stay away. Della was my problem and mine alone.

"I saw your daughter on StreamVid today," I said. "You really fucked up your kids, you know?"

"No less than my parents fucked me up," she said. "No less than your parents fucked you up."

"They didn't fuck me up," I said. "But you certainly tried to."

"It's not too late, you know," Della said. "You can get the book and bring me back."

"No, thanks," I said.

The palmetto bug returned, crawling slowly on a path only it knew of. Its shining brown body was slow and sluggish as it inched between me and the rotting corpse of my former online friend. I positioned my foot over the insect. "It's time for you to go."

"But wait! I have this amazing idea..."

Crunch.

The brittle exoskeleton collapsed under the weight of my shoe. I glanced back up, and Della was gone — for how long this time, I wasn't sure. Somehow, this time it felt a little more final. I smiled, straightened out my graduation gown, and walked toward the gathering crowd, where my real friends and family were waiting for me.

About the Author

Wendy Dalrymple loves to explore the beauty in horrific things. She holds a BA in Journalism from The University of South Florida and is a member of the HWA. When she's not writing Florida Gothic horror, you can find her hiking with her family, painting (bad) wall art, and trying to grow as many pineapples as possible. Follow her on Twitter @wendy_dalrymple.

Also by Wendy Dalrymple

Don't Read This or You Might Die
THIS BOOK IS DEFINITELY CURSED.

You probably shouldn't read it. Looks like you're going to anyway.

Don't say I didn't warn you...

Hannah Howarth has always wanted to land a coveted internship at Visage Magazine. It's clear from her very first day working at Visage that she doesn't fit in and is looked down upon by the Editor in Chief, Grace, and her legion of intimidating, fashionable staff writers.

Hannah tries her best to fit in, but when she is tasked with studying the magazine's special training manual, it becomes clear that there's more than meets the eye to her new job. Hannah grapples with her past as more and more strange and unsettling occurrences plunge her head-first into a living nightmare.

Girls' Night Out
It was just supposed to be a girls' night out...

Stay-at-home mom Kris loves her life and her family but she can't help but feel as though she's lost a little bit of herself. Sometimes it feels like she could burst out of her own skin. She's starving for attention, starving for an escape and starving to reclaim her own sense of identity and place in the world again.

On a rare girls' night out, Kris has a little too much to drink and gets roughed up and romanced by a hypnotic stranger. She goes home with a wounded shoulder and an equally wounded ego, and wakes up the following day with strange new cravings. With every day, Kris finds it more and more difficult to deny that something is terribly wrong with her.

With the help of a new friend, Kris soon learns that she'll have to make the biggest sacrifice of all if she wants to keep her family and herself intact. Girls Night Out is a fever dream dissection of how one bad decision and a lifetime of repression and regrets can lead to a spiral self-destruction.

Printed in the USA
CPSIA information can be obtained
at www.ICGtesting.com
LVHW070430280923
759395LV00004B/51